# Early Men

# Early Men

## Stories

Britt Haraway

LITERARY PRESS
LAMAR UNIVERSITY

ISBN: 978-1-942956-25-9
Library of Congress Control Number: 2016947524


Manufactured in the United States
Book Design: Theresa L. Ener
Author Photo: Ale Alfaro


Lamar University Literary Press
Beaumont, Texas

# Acknowledgments

I feel profound gratitude for my family and friends who supported me throughout the writing process. My mom Susan Arrison and my dad Claude Haraway are my first friends and mentors ... thank you. Mike and Mary Anne have shown me much kindness and support over the years, as have my siblings Ashley, Drew, Chip, and Marti. Thank you to all the people that helped me read and edit these stories, including Rick and Steve Barthelme, Mary Robison, Sara Brady, Jerry Craven, Jon Raymond, Jean Braithwaite, and Josh Weil. Most especially thank you to Emmy Pérez for your care and intelligence and for adding Joaquín and Anaís to our journey.

Thanks also to the editors who published previous versions of these stories. "Horses and Tea" first appeared in *The South Dakota Review*. "Germantown Players Club" was published in *BorderSenses*. "Wall Doxey" first appeared in *New Madrid*.

Fiction from Lamar University Literary Press

David Bowles, *Border Lore*
Kevin Casey, *Four Peace*
Terry Dalrymple, *Love Stories, Sort Of*
Gerald Duff, *Memphis Mojo*
Gretchen Johnson, *The Joy of Deception*
Christopher Linforth, *When You Find Us We Will Be Gone*
Tom Mack and Andrew Geyer, editors, *A Shared Voice*
Harold Raley, *Louisiana Rogue*
Jim Sanderson, *Trashy Behavior*
Jan Seale, *Appearances*
Melvin Sterne, *The Number You Have Reached*
John Wegner, *Love is not a Dirty Word and Other Stories*
Robert Wexelblatt, *The Artist Wears Rough Clothing*

For more information about these and other books, go to
www.lamar.edu/literarypress

# CONTENTS

# Bad Joke Bob

Knoxville used to be a hometown for me, but that week it was just the next sales stop, all aboard, the best postal equipment made. I went up to my hotel room and needed a friendly voice, so I called old Ronnie up. I could tell he wanted to avoid an evening with me, but I pushed right past all that. To think, he must've intentionally left my name off the invitation list for his wedding, and then tries to squirm his way out of a measly little dinner. I introduced them, for Christ's sake! Don't think I haven't noticed you married the girl. My mom had forwarded me the announcement from the paper and I wrote a damn toast out for it. No invitation. Priceless words, stories that would make mothers laugh through tears.

It wasn't the first time someone tried to cull me out. Bob Sanderson is my name, but for most of my life I've had nicknames. Pinocchio, the Throw-Up Kid, Skinny Pimp, and Bad Joke Bob. Ronnie said the most recent on the phone, and I just stared out the hotel room window at a fat cumulus cloud gathering all the moisture it could. My senior year it rained more in Knoxville than it did in Seattle. I wrote this fact in my notes and would use it the next day at my sales meeting. People like that sort of thing. To be reminded of how strange weather can be.

It was hard to grow up without my proper name. At

least, I made it hard at first. To lie in my room and hope the day got snowed. I listened to a kid two years younger tell a girl on the bus that she shouldn't sit down there because a month prior I had puked all over the bus, all over people. *My appendix exploded, asshole.* They don't understand, and my mother asked, why are you in your room all the time, and why don't you spend the night with some friends? *I threw up on them, Mother.* You have to have courage, son, and patience. I hate school, and don't let them bully you, and the rest. If your father were here, he'd show you what to do. If he were here instead of California, he'd show you how to punch and kick, but he'd be wrong, in his special brand of wrongness. She'd be holding my hand, squeezing it on the emotional points in the sentence like the dying do on TV. You have to turn your cheek, she said, and learn to belong.

To belong in college all it took was to be a stooge, to help the fraternity brothers meet girls. I remembered when Ronnie asked me for an introduction to Sarah. She was sitting on the stool at a bar in front of a large mirror flanked by three light bulbs on each side. She had jet-black hair that shined in the strong light; it curled to her shoulders, and her eyes were the color of rusty pennies.

It was not really a trick at all. I just went up to her and started talking. Since the girls like Sarah weren't interested in me, it smoothed things out for the Ronnie types who stumbled into their successes without ever needing to scan the pavement for banana peels. After me, a pressed-out anxious version of me, the guy would appear charming in light. The girl would send every possible signal that they weren't enjoying my company, but I would keep on, and when the guy would tell me to get lost, they'd have that instant credibility you feel when the lie was the thing you wanted to hear.

It had stopped raining by the time I found Sarah and Ronnie's, and there was a smell in the air—old dust, ancient. Sarah was standing at the door and seemed friendly. Old Ronnie had lucked out, it seemed. They had a big house and I'd gotten lost enough on the way over to see the lake a few times. It sprawled out, carving out these cul-de-sac type neighborhoods hugging around it. Sarah said there was something familiar about me when she introduced herself.

I said, "Well, ma'am, you might remember—"

"The cover of *Time* magazine, right, Bob," Ronnie said from behind her. I couldn't see his face in the door's shadow, but he sounded the same. More friendly than on the phone. Ronnie reached across her to give me a hand-shake and put his other hand on her shoulder.

"Oh yes," I said. "That cover was everywhere. Some folks were surprised to see that a salesman won man of the year. Just don't realize how popular we are."

"That right?" Sarah said and turned back to Ronnie and smiled.

"Hell, yes," I said and spread my feet apart and made hand gestures at each point. "I can prove it. Now, Ronnie tells me you work deeds and trusts in a law office, right?"

"Yes, sir," she said.

"I bet you have a lot of mail that goes out, and it needs to go out quick, I expect."

"You bet," Sarah said quick, like she knew I needed

11

her to keep it going.

"Well the ticket for you, and your firm, is a brand new X-14RR mailer. This thing pumps 'um out every second with the metered mail in the right corner just like a picture. Why, you can make it fold and seal the mail all by its—"

Sarah couldn't seem to hold back her laugh.

"Oh, I see. You were hoping that would be your wedding present. We'll see if I can work out a discount," I said. I rubbed my chin as if considering and they both laughed a little.

Ronnie showed me around the house, which had art prints on the wall, no originals, but all had frames. The bathroom down the hall was filled with those potpourri leaf baskets, which are good coverers—cinnamon. He pointed down a dark L-shaped turn in the hall and told me their bedroom was just down there. I wondered if it is impolite to look in a couple's bedroom. I just said it looked like he had a great house. He led me back through the living room that had a couch and two recliners facing a big TV. One of the chairs was by the fireplace and had a floor lamp beside it. The other was worn brown leather, maybe passed down from a grandfather; I'm sure Ronnie mentioned having a grandfather once. The chair was next to a small table with a do-it-all remote on it, and I figured that was where Ronnie sat. He walked through the living room and took a left into the kitchen, where he started unscrewing a bottle of wine with a tool I was not familiar with.

Through the sliding glass door, I saw Sarah leaning against the deck rail, and she called for me to join her. The deck wood was deep brown, stained from the weather. The cold front had driven through and left behind a clear sky perfect for stargazers like me. Venus would be out tonight following the moon around like a blue diamond, but however solid it looked, the storms raged. Orion would make its first appearance in months, and the scopes would show Betelgeuse, the hunter's red giant armpit. It was dying, probably only five billion years to go. The sun would go red by then, but you could count the seasons by Orion.

"You keeping all the property in the right names?" I asked her.

"Oh, sometimes. People want to see how much they can get now and what they'll get when the others are gone. How about you? How is life on the road?"

"All right. It turns out I'm pretty good at this stuff. Almost don't know what to do with myself. I could sell snow to a polar bear." There was a pause and I said, "Looks like y'all got a nice life here. Love the North Shore. Some folks complain about TVA damming all the rivers. But if you put a little boat out there in the middle, far enough from these deck lights, you'll see the Milky Way swing out, a big swath of a thousand stars. Prettier than anything we could make."

"Is that right? We'll have to get us a boat. You could give us the tour," she said. There was something deep in her eyes, like you could throw something in there, and it wouldn't make a sound. I do this thing sometimes when I meet a nice person, start to thinking about how they are perfect, and I feel myself being surprised, knowing I shouldn't be. Especially a lawyer. All my lawyers jokes were bad. Well, they were good. But the lawyers bad. I looked over my shoulder and saw Ronnie walking towards me; he held three empty glasses by the stems in one hand and the bottle in the other. I wondered about thinking about his wife when he was not around.

"Ronnie, Bob here says you need to buy me a boat for Christmas," Sarah said.

Ronnie gave me a glass and went over and handed one to Sarah. "Oh, he's full of ideas. Selling boats now too, Bob?" He put his hands around her waist and stood behind her. His chin rested on the top of her head, and they looked like they fit. I looked down and there was a spider crawling next to a dead mosquito. Not much in a mosquito—poison, and some of my blood. I discreetly squashed them both and looked at the couple. They looked so relaxed I wondered if wine could work that fast.

"Y'all fit together like a couple of Legos. I'd like to give y'all my official congratulations on your nuptials." I raised my glass, and he nodded.

"I hate you couldn't be there," she said.

Hated what? Seemed like a clear case of premeditated uninvitation to me.

"Things don't always work out." I smelled the wine, swirling it around. It smelled bitter, like it might be too close to vinegar. They didn't say anything and swayed as if the moon and Venus pulled them both, and I tried to let the silence marinate, but eventually I pretended I needed to check my phone and walked away.

In high school, they called me Skinny Pimp. No dates back in those days and always skinny—they weren't far off, the clever cusses. I'd made the doubly stupid decision to become the mascot, which increased the attention on me but not in a socially helpful way. I tried hard, dedicated myself to being a credible Conquistador. I wasn't sure why our high school was the Conquistadors. Apparently the Spanish had done the best job mapping the Tennessee River Valley. To me it meant strutting around the sidelines with a sword with the permission to do any outrageous thing you wanted because you believed from the first that you were right. It was how I thought of all the men that had been in my life. They were slayers and self-righteous and generally had a lot of cultural success. It felt wonderful to be in those clothes, until I realized it was just me in the fake muscles—only the idea of me having power made people feel so amused. In the halls the guys would ask, how many hotties did you bang after the game, skinny? I hoped maybe they would forget the joke but they didn't and turned their school rings backwards and knotted my skull, which started to resemble the Alps. And I would try to smile and josh with them, showing I was on the same team, but in my room at night, I turned the music loud to distract me and asked the question, how do I get out of this? The song I liked was called "Territorial Pissings." It said, "Just because you're paranoid, doesn't mean they're not after you." This was said very loud in a tone I could appreciate.

Sarah broke the silence, calling me over. "Tell me, Bob. Why did they call you that? I kind of like your jokes."

"In the fraternity?" I asked.

"Yeah, why Bad Joke Bob?" she asked.

Ronnie straightened his knees and said, "Long story, huh, Bob. I'm ready for some chow."

Three train whistles blew, and I looked south like I could see it coming down the line. I thought of asking if people who live by trains really do get used to the noise.

Sarah increased her volume and said, "I almost smacked Ronnie when he called you that."

"I don't care much." It was fun to yell the words. "If you participate and make it yours, it doesn't sting so bad. Like taking the initiative to dive into cold water." There was a pause as the train moved on, and I said, "It was easy, is easier."

"They don't even sound like jokes really."

"Some are better than others."

"Is that even you, though, what silly frat guys say?" Either her stare made me nervous, or her questions did. She must have sensed my tension, because she said, "Tell us a good one."

That wasn't too hard. "There was this woman at the b—"

Ronnie said, "None of those old fraternity ones, Bob. I'm getting pretty hungry."

"This was last night. At the bar, I was sitting by this woman, and the Olympics were on. A swimmer from UT held up a medal: the five-hundred-meter butterfly."

"Jim Sexton, right?" Sarah asked.

"Yeah, I think so. Anyway, during the commercial, I told this smart-looking woman that I used to swim against the guy. That seemed to impress her, so I told her about how I had been in the SEC title race with him, same event. We were at a dead heat to the last turn when all of a sudden I got a thought—butterflies don't swim. Damn things wouldn't last thirty seconds in the water. I told her I swam the rest of the way in dog- paddle and finished dead last."

Sarah asked, "Is that a joke?"

"Well, she gave a little laugh. Excused herself, though, to the other end where there was a smaller TV. Maybe the action was too intense on the big screen."

Sarah shook her head and said, let's eat. Ronnie was eager and opened the sliding door and went inside. She walked after him, but stopped at the door and said, "It's a good story, Bob." She went into the house.

I stayed outside a moment and grabbed a rock from the gravel at the bottom of the steps and threw it at the lake. Ripples swept out in circles; it was instant, like the water was totally prepared. Stars know all about circles too, use all different shapes of them. Spiral, ellipse, one called strange. It's funny how they knew about circles before we did. Like the first person who made a wheel—that must've been a popular person.

I walked through the door, and the smell doubled my hunger. The breakfast table sat between the back of the kitchen and the glass door to the deck. The wall that separated the kitchen and the living room ended before the breakfast area, but I could still see the backs of the two recliners. Ronnie must sit there yelling at the TV when the Vols played, calling the coach a chicken shit. Sarah would have her light on over her shoulder reading something with headphones on. They might be worlds apart those days, but she'd look up from her page and smile at his anger. He would ask, "Did you see that crap?" Once he saw her smile, the anger, which was real at first, would become mocking. I wondered how he got her to accept such a contract.

I stared around the room and saw the rectangular frames of three Van Gogh prints. Ronnie came to the table

17

with another bottle of wine and sat to my left. Sarah came with a casserole that she put in the middle of the table; she sat down opposite of me.

"Dig in," Sarah said. "Especially you. You look like you need some fat."

"Too much hotel food, I guess." We all began eating in silence. I don't know why that bothered me, but after five minutes, I pointed to the Van Gogh prints and said, "Now, *that's* orange. Pretty much demolishes your boys on any game day." I dropped my fork on the floor tiles and it hit like a bell. "I'm sorry," I said. "You can't take me anywhere."

Sarah excused me and went to the kitchen to get another fork.

"Cut his ear," Ronnie said. "No guts. Our boys can take him."

"Ha!" Sarah said loudly from the kitchen.

"That one with the man in the wheat field; it looks like the stalks are grabbing at him." I looked at Ronnie.

"What you need is positivity. They look like waves." He took a bite. "Like surfing."

Sarah handed me the fork and looked me in the eye; I winked.

"This comes to you from a man who's never been alone," I said, leaning back in my chair.

"How's that?" Ronnie asked with his fork in mid-air.

"Don't you see he's lonely? Look. The ocean doesn't know who you are. It just swallows you up."

"Whatever," Ronnie said.

"Ronnie likes to become twelve when he is contra-

18

dicted," Sarah said. "That's good though. I don't think the nickname will work when you talk like that."

I tried very hard to think.

She said, "What did you really want to say when those boys told you your jokes were so bad?"

"I guess . . . I don't know." I looked down at the plate. "Why they didn't make their own?" I said and she nodded.

Sarah squinted her eyes like she understood.

"You were a good clown, Bob. Our sweet little old clown," Ronnie said, taking another bite.

I slammed my hands to the table. The force rattled the glasses.

There was silence until Sarah spoke. "In France, their clowns are sad."

Ronnie took a drink and said, "Dumbo jumped off a building into a glass of water."

I gripped my hair between my fingers and tried to calm the nerves that shot through me. There were so many I thought I would cry.

I stood up and spoke as if the room were filled with guests. "Ladies and gentlemen. We are here tonight to salute these two amazing people, who are very important to me. Their meeting, in truth, was my only good joke. Let me tell you about this guy Ronnie."

Ronnie stood up, knocking his chair to the ground, and yelled, "Sit, Bob. I said sit!"

"I have blundered my way so many times, I feel as though I may never get back to even," I said.

"I said shut it, Bob!"

"This guy was a real water juggler, as they say. It

19

wasn't a little black book he was writing. 'It's an important trilogy,' he used to say. I first I met Sarah in a b—"

Ronnie's fist connected squarely on my lips, parted, and my teeth dug into the soft side of my lips. I hit my lower back on the top of the chair; it turned over, and I fell, bleeding, on the linoleum, staring at a ceiling fan.

"What the fuck, Ronnie?" Sarah said, standing up.

"I warned him."

My face felt fat, and my eyes had watered. My mouth tasted like I was chewing gum with the aluminum foil still on. As my head began to clear, I wondered if my lips would get any fatter. Why? It had been an evening filled with glory.

And then I realized he thought I might tell about the girls he met after Sarah. But it was not going to be a bad toast but a good one. I struggled to my feet.

"Are you all right, Bob?" Sarah asked and handed me a dishtowel with ice in it she must have gotten when I was down.

"Fine, ma'am, but I didn't get to finish my toast." I picked up a glass with a broken stem from the floor and spit in it the color of wine.

"Try it, asshole. You'll be on the ground if you say another—" Ronnie said.

"I wrote this toast, and I'm not leaving until you hear it," I said.

"Someone better talk," she said. "What's this about, Ronnie?"

He sat down. It was apparent that she was on the side of the injured. He stared at the white linen cloth and traced its patterns.

Sarah looked over at me. "Bob?"

I looked away from her down at Ronnie. "Every man should spend one night alone or, at least, on the couch." I raised my glass and talked as if I was at a podium. "This couple is my only good joke. Back in the fraternity days, I was a real sport. I'd take one for the team. Throw myself on the grenade, you might say, anyhow. Remember, Ronnie?" I raised my glass to him. "He leaned over my shoulder and pointed to Sarah at the bar. 'That's the one, Bad Joke Bob. I need the magic show tonight.' Finally, Ronnie made the right call. Much better than when we found him drunk with the Sigma Chi pet goat, eh Ronnie. You, Sarah." I raised my glass to her.

She walked over to the glass door and stared out at the lake. She didn't say anything or look at either of us, and Ronnie's eyes never left the linen. I finished with saying, "You are a special person and we are happy to welcome you into our hearts. I know these two will have one of those special marriages we'll all watch and admire. To true friends and true love." I raised my glass and hoped one of them would look at me and know how much I meant the words.

Sarah turned to me. She had her arms crossed and her lips pinched; she was clenching her jaw. She said, "What's up Ronnie?"

"He's probably embarrassed that he misled you," I said, wondering the extent of the real story.

I started to say more and she held up her finger.

"No, Bob, no more. I asked him before about the whole good cop, bad cop thing. So right now, I want you to know why Ronnie is hitting you."

Ronnie let out a sigh and kept moving his finger in circles.

"In fact, Bob, can you give us some space," she said.

I walked over to Sarah and put a hand on her shoulder, and she put her hand up in a stop sign. I whispered the words, "Thank you." When I pulled my hand away there was a spot of blood on her patterned dress, and I wondered if I would ever see her again. As I passed Ronnie, I said thanks to him too, and out of the corner of my eye, I saw his remote control. I reached down, picked it up, and walked out of the house. There seemed a quiet to the whole world. The house, the yard, I was surprised I couldn't feel the earth spinning; no planes were in the air. I looked up, and the stars seemed to have multiplied, fattened; the humidity must be lower. Some were older and put off light even before the Milky Way was born. Some three times as big, whole galaxies that look like a dot, burning so much they'd collapse in on themselves. I looked east to where the moon would come up. I remembered there was a public dock off the road on the way out. It would be a nice place to watch it.

## Knoxville Dead

Hedwig was my German instructor, but in her class I learned very little language. Her class usually consisted of a fifty-minute discussion about the unjustified conflict in Iraq, German skepticism of modern war, and Europe's new friendliness. Her arguments were tenacious and filled with earnest sentiment, and after a while, even my Republican friend Andy had stopped raising his hand to yeah but, *ich denk dass du ...*

I'd go back to my room at my mom's house and imagine Hedwig seething at night, when other people say prayers, thinking of every possible defense of the war, finding holes in this so-called thinking, and improvising ways to blow them up. In her disgust of the American military, she was a lot like my mother, but her reasons were more compelling, the nerves all real and raw.

When we started dating, I dropped out of school because she felt bad every time my name came up on her roll. First, I'd asked her to get coffee, where she told me that her husband was fighting in Iraq. After I told her that didn't make sense, although it did, she agreed and said that her family in Germany was embarrassed that her husband, John, was part of the war.

Next, I took her on a hike up Clingman's Dome in

23

the Smoky Mountains. At that time of year, the leaves in Tennessee were yellow and red, and everyone drove there to see them. Most people never got out of their cars, but Hedwig and I did. We hiked for hours and picked up fallen leaves and studied them, holding them up to the sun so we could read through them. We compared the veins and the way the best ones branched and would line up if you folded them over. At the top of the mountain, there was a lodge where we lunched, and she told me a story about getting yelled at recently at a soldier's funeral, a friend of her and John's, because she was German and was taken for a protestor, which she was *not* on that day.

We held hands on the wooden bench and sipped from the wine I packed in and we agreed that the Smoky Mountains were aptly named, but that some lost tribe probably had a similar meaning name, only more beautiful said out loud. I was ashamed that I could not tell her what tribe used to live there and maybe still did. She said Clingman's Dome had no ring to it, but more like someone was selling tires.

The next week, we celebrated Oktoberfest in Knoxville's Old City. Both of us got drunk accidentally, and she told me she missed the summers near Hanover where she had learned to play in country streams with her grandmother. I told her I had liked camping with my dad in that part of Tennessee and that I'd secretly thought about him on our hike and wished I'd brought some of his ashes. I told her I hated the way my mother had turned our house into a museum of my dead father and sister. She said that part of being German was being scared of what you'll learn at the museum.

24

We were next to Lucile's, a small jazz club that looked crowded and wonderfully loud. I grabbed her arm to stop her from going in. She had her hair tied up in a bun with two sticks. I took them out and ran my hand through her hair. She said she missed her husband, and we kissed.

———

The next week over dinner I told Mama about Hedwig and John. She said it was good that I was finally getting out of the house.

Mama and I were washing the dishes after supper with the news on, coming from a handheld receiver that followed my mom from room to room of an evening. A woman was talking affectionately about the meteor shower that week. "So, look up once in a while. Just before dawn and you'll see fireworks sailing across the sky."

"Oh please," Mama said and handed me a dish to dry. Her black hair was streaked with silver, and her thin lips looked hard in the fluorescent light that came from over the kitchen island. She'd been meaning to change the fixture but hadn't. Dad had always gone cheap on those kinds of things.

I stacked the dishes in a wooden hutch that he had brought back from his stint in Korea. It was an antique painted with thin gold lines that curled and laced. The wood had a smell that I'd enjoyed since being a boy, imagining ancient trees and my parents young.

The war report was next, and they led off with a civilian casualty report. Over 110,000 regular people dead.

"Can you imagine?" I asked and leaned over and turned it up.

"Turn it off." Mama turned it off herself, set it on the counter, and then picked it up again and took out the batteries. "That filth in Washington. Bunch of widow makers." For some reason, she blamed Dad and Lynn's deaths on the military, although they had only been driving home from the base. Mom had been going to the psychologist to talk about this.

"So many," I said. "I didn't see it coming."

"Nothing registers with you," Mama said and walked out of the room. I leaned against the counter. The glasses were drying upside down on a towel and were forming clouds, so I turned them right side up. I tried to get my head around that number. Freshman year, I'd gone to the UT-Alabama game and the Vols had won. That crowd had been over 107,000. On game days, Neyland Stadium was the fifth-largest city in Tennessee, and when that Alabama boy fumbled, we went crazy. If we had all disappeared, died in some freak Oak Ridge explosion, there would've been such an outcry. It would've made quite an impression.

————

Hedwig had a Dachshund named Helmut. It had recently won the local dog show, and Hedwig and I were taking it to the vet even though it wasn't sick. It wiggled in my lap and propped its paws on the armrest when she turned off the engine. I held it like I would a baby, its ribs hard under its short coat. Helmut turned and licked my face.

"She starts to like you," Hedwig said.

"Does your vet know John?" I asked, wondering if I should stay in the car.

"Vets and neighbors are largely indifferent people to me. It's mine to worry." She grabbed the dog and got out.

I took short, quick strides to catch her before she went in the office. She went to the expensive vet. It was on a good size piece of land well away from the road. It looked like a farm, the office, ranch style and wooden with a horse and a Lab painted on the side of the house. Up the path, a Bulldog was happily barking, scraping its claws on some new fencing. It stepped on a muddy Shih Tzu to get closer to us, the dogs following each other back and forth, closer to Hedwig, closer to me. "I'm no pro at this."

She came closer to me and said something soft and playful to the dog in German. "We like Colins, don't we Helmut. He's a youth." Sometimes she made my name plural, like there were several of me. She touched my face, and it was the first time she'd been so nice to me in public since we'd been drinking that night. It felt good to have her and the dog all kind of wedged together at the farm. She had gotten her hair cut recently and had bangs now. I pushed some hair towards her ear, but it wouldn't reach behind and so just fell back there like before.

———

I didn't stay with Hedwig that night, because Mama and I had a date to watch the meteors. I walked up the stairs and went into Mama's room. She was lying in bed, her head between two pillows. I stood in front of her closet but didn't know what to say. Her clothes were all organized by color and style. She was a vice president in a management company, in charge of fifty employees, and organization, she often said, helped her make it to the weekends. She was getting rid of Dad's stuff one by one, but his green Air Force winter jacket was still in the corner. I traced the name on the front, then unhooked it and threw it on the bed.

She still had his guitar hanging on the wall where he'd kept it. He would write these little songs when I was younger, about our family. One time, Dad and Mom sang together at her work picnic when Lynn and I were little. Mom had feathered fly-backs framing her face and was looking over my dad's shoulder following the lyrics. "So baby, be a friend to me." His songs were always too friendly. It's how I remember my parents now, like a couple of nerds. Mom used to do more of that, things like singing in front of people.

I found her wool hat, too, and threw it at the pillow covering her head.

"Quit it." She peeked through.

"We're going to the roof and watch the stars."

She sighed like a teenager but sat up.

I went to my room to get some warm clothes. She met me in the hall, and we climbed out the window onto the roof. We walked carefully across the roof, as if it were a frozen pond, and lay down.

After a while, I hadn't seen anything fall, but the sky looked nice. Knoxville was throwing up a sheen that cut the sky by half, but I was glad we were on the roof, waiting. Broadway, the street to the north, was lined with strip malls and Taco Bells, and I heard the hum of tires and traffic. Mama was reading a book by James Agee that said Broadway used to be a quiet street.

Mama had on two coats, Dad's green jacket outside and baggy. She said, "We could see but for these lights. If I had a bat large enough." She swung her arms, still lying down. "I'd start with all the orange ones. Then that tower out there. It would blink its last."

"I'd relieve you when you tuckered out," I said.

"You'd be around, as always," she said.

There was a pause and I thought about it. How most twenty-two-year-olds would've moved out and moved on to their own life. At first, I knew Mama needed me. Maybe she did, or I wanted her to need me. I said, "We're sunbathing—all these suns at night. Put on the Buffett and pass the lotion." The stars were pinpricks in all that space; it was like you'd choke.

She pointed to Orion and his dog. "They're friends."

I'd always thought that was funny—a man and a dog. In Lit. class, we'd read a book that said clichés started for their "effective locution."

She put her arm back in the thick coat.

"I heard they are going to put bombs up there," I said.

"Cassiopeia, how does that story go?" she asked. It shined blue against the black.

I had been majoring in Greek for a while and part

29

of the constellation was her in a torture chair, but I didn't say it out loud. They'd been talking about torture a lot on the news, and I didn't want to set Mama off. I shrugged my shoulders, and it made a sandpaper noise against the shingles, so I kept doing it. "Seems calm up there, but it's all galaxies and stars smashing into each other, black holes, taking all you can."

"Your dad liked that one, had called it 'the big W,'" she said. "He said Dub-yu like the president does."

"I know," I said. My dad and sister got hit by a semi on the way back from where he was stationed in Virginia. She had flown out to meet him and ride back with Dad to have some time alone. She had been having a hard time and started doing harder drugs, and Dad was good at that kind of talk—pointed and fair. The last two years had been hard on Mama. "Mama, did I ever tell you about the night Dad, Lynn and me sang together?" She sat still, and I lay down and huddled back. The edges of my jacket covered my cheeks. "This song came on in the car and he started singing. Lynn sang, too, and beat time on his arm, and he got louder."

"Did you sing?" she asked. Her eyes were closed and the first shooting star came by—a small one, a piece of sand but fast and bright.

"It didn't mean much to me then."

Mama groaned.

"I moved my lips a little." Looking back, the moment was so intact. I knew everything about the song and them. There was nothing else that could have happened at that moment. Trying to tell somebody about it was like a punch line, empty and predictable. I started to wonder if Mama and I could ever have that kind of evening again.

"You've always been embarrassed," she said.

"I should be a squirrel. Look up, and not notice stars."

Mama shrugged and didn't say anything. A shooting star came left to right and she pointed and said, "I can't tell if I want you to go or stay."

"We're supposed to make a wish, Mama," I said. "Imagine where the radiant entered and make a wish."

"I know, baby. That's what I did," she said and scooted over and laid her head on my shoulder.

I wondered if she was wishing that she could bring strange men to the house, guessing it was time she might want to. She had plenty of years left. They can keep you alive a long time these days. Time enough for a couple of lives. She and Dad never got to be the next them, me and Lynn gone.

———

A few weeks later, Mama invited Hedwig for dinner. I picked Hedwig up at her and John's place. She let me in and asked me to wait for her to get ready.

"Remember, we're a casual bunch," I said. There was *Star* magazine on the glass coffee table in front of the couch. I picked it up, thumbed through it, but the German didn't seem to be in the present tense, the one I knew. I was in a small living room with green shag carpet. Through the door, there was a guest bathroom and then another living

31

room with a bar.

She came back with a silver necklace in her hand. "Will you get this on?" she asked and held up her hair. I kissed her and smelled her shampoo.

It took me a few tries and she asked me to hurry.

"I've been meaning to ask, Hedwig." I finally got it latched, and she turned. "Why do you have two living rooms?"

"One for us. One for the children." She clapped her hands once and asked, "Well, how do I look?"

"What's the word for 'beautiful'?" I asked.

"You are a poor student." She smoothed my jacket and gave me a hug, and I scratched her back with my right hand.

I asked, "Y'all plan to have kids, then?"

She pulled away and got her purse from the coat rack by the door. "John wanted to wait until he get back."

I nodded and felt this big silence in the big house.

We went out to the car and I started driving, thinking we were like some old couple just off for a drive. She lived out on Alcoa Highway, which was prettier than Broadway. The road bisects two ridges covered with old trees. Before the bridge over the Tennessee River, she said, "See that island." On the edge of the water, a small hill jutted out. "A great many American egrets nest there." Up in the trees, dozens of nests rested in the crooks of the branches. The sun was going down, and I could see their outlines, like clumps of shredded cheese. "John says on the island they have less predators."

I nodded and looked to the right at Neyland Stadium next to the water. It was tall and wide and made with white iron support beams that crossed at different angles. A nice industrial look. One hundred thousand people. The count would've been higher by then. I kept straight at the end of the bridge towards home.

"You should stay with me and Helmut for a while," Hedwig said.

I stared at her. She was blowing on her nails and then looked up.

"Red!" she said and pointed at the light.

I hit the brakes and we both rocked forward and backward. "I never even thought about doing that," I said, and I didn't know what to say after that.

Mama had everything ready by the time we got there. She'd prepared three courses continental style. Earlier, as Mama and I put the food together, I'd told her not to try and be German about dinner, but the meal appealed to her sense of progression and order.

Mama gave Hedwig a businessman's handshake. Being a foot shorter, Mama looked older, but nice with her professional smile on. She led Hedwig to the head of the table. I sat too and Mama poured the wine into one of the three glasses we had in front of us. Hedwig swirled her wine around and tilted it up to the light. It looked like dirty windows.

"Very good bottle," Hedwig said.

"Around the Rhine," Mama said. She took up a bowl, part of her Korean china, and dished out a thick stew. "Is that your river?"

"It is much west of Hanover. I had the Leine. I would swim in summers."

33

"Did you know you used to could swim on campus?" I said. "Trout fish right in Third Creek on campus. Now they have signs that say 'bio-hazard.'"

"This is the river from the Civil War?" Hedwig asked.

"I think so." There was a battle in the Civil War near campus. All the students live in a neighborhood called The Fort, which once had a real meaning.

My mother was shaking her head. "All wars are civil wars."

"This means nice, 'civil'?" Hedwig asked me.

"She means that people are fighting their own people."

"I'm sorry," Mama said with emotion. "Your husband is in that awful place."

"It must be strange to you that I … I am married but I spend time with Colins." Hedwig's napkin covered her mouth, making the words muffled.

"It is hard to be married to the military." Mama stared at the tablecloth, gathering it up then smoothing it out. "They make you alone."

Hedwig looked like she would cry.

I looked at Mama and wondered about the part of her life that I knew nothing about. That she had been a woman much like Hedwig, resilient despite fear. That the affection from Skype or the telephone could not be satisfying. In Mama's day, people sent each other cassette tapes. It was hard to imagine my parents sitting there talking into the machines in an empty room. And I forgave Mother her secret life, even as I recognized that such a gesture was not in my power. While I didn't want to know anything more, her actions must've been natural, and my attitude surprised me. How much more would Hedwig teach me about the world? And how would it be to roam in her house and learn it the way you do, where you go towards the kitchen or a ringing phone without ever thinking about where it is?

Mama started to eat again, but dropped her knife and fork, which rang on the plate. "It's awful. Family is the real thing they break. You give them your guts, the best years you've got, and they take more. Keep on; we'll give you this. Five more years, we'll pay you back eventually. Hah." She twisted her hair in a rope and let go.

Outside, it started raining. I got up and looked out the window. The neighbor was walking his dog. They both had on yellow coats. "He's walking the dog," I said.

Hedwig said, "If people would only talk more. Certainly 9/11 was unfair. But also, global economic is unfair. If the world would only say this to each other."

I turned and leaned on an empty seat that used to be Lynn's place and said, "We need people like my dad and John. There will always be wars. Nothing to do about that."

"Eat or be eaten, huh," Mama said. "Where's the heart in that, boy?"

"He is just a man, Mrs. Klemm," Hedwig said and cut off some meat from the bone. She brushed it through some juice on her plate. "If only there more women."

They laughed and I sat down. I started to eat but poured another glass of wine instead. "I'm going to stay with Hedwig for a while, Mama."

Mama clapped. She reached over and tugged my neck. She kissed her own palm and touched hands with

Hedwig.

"You don't have to be that excited," I said.

Still with Hedwig's hand Mama said, "You don't know. I'm not a bad mother." Mama breathed hard and crunched up. Hedwig rubbed the back of her hand, warming it. "Every time I look at him, I see my husband and my girl."

———————

When Hedwig got home one day after work, she was standoffish and worried and said she needed to be cheered up. They had a record player in the kids' living room, so I led her to the couch and put on a jazz record. It was the local guy we'd heard in town our first night together. I started dancing with a pillow from the couch and said, "No one has ever danced like this in this very spot." I dipped the pillow low.

She stood up and took the pillow from me. She went to push me, and I turned, making it a dance step. We danced, and she put her head on my collarbone. It felt warm and I realized she was crying. I tried dancing harder, spinning her away from me. She let go of my hand and sat back down. I sat with my legs under the glass coffee table.

She said, "He's wanting to accept another tour."

I didn't know what to say. I hadn't planned on getting involved in anything like that. The table was dirty with Helmut smudges on it in the afternoon light. One looked like a male fingerprint on it, bigger than Hedwig's. Bending closer, I pressed my thumb down next to it, and when I compared them, it was too big to be mine.

She smiled at me. "You will clean it now like Helmut. With your tongue."

"What if I still love you when he comes back?" I asked.

A faster track came on, so she got up and turned it off. She sat down behind me and rested her chin on the soft part of my shoulder.

————

Hedwig had class almost every day, and I got into the habit of wandering through the house and coming upon her and John's things. I'd gotten a job at night at the pizza place in the old part of the city. On my days off, I played with Helmut or went into John's shop in the back yard, which was a metal shed with a green Plexiglas roof that must've been a greenhouse at one point. He worked metal with a torch and propane and had built a human body out of car parts. After he got through with the war, he was going to use the money to finish med school, so the man's body was anatomically proportional. He was a medic out there already. In the desert. The body's heart was the head of a piston, and its liver was a bent oil pan. I ran my fingers along the body, and the welding was smooth.

In Hedwig's bedroom, I came upon a letter that John had sent her and wanted to read it but stopped at seeing the picture. John was a big guy. His helmet was tucked under his arm like a football player's. He would make an imposing kids' doctor. He had the makings of a full beard and held a machine gun pointed down, looking rugged next to a famous-looking Persian painting. He was looking over it like it was already his, like it was something he could just borrow and pocket. Like a place was something you could put in a picture and then send off in the envelope that could be carried.

I wondered what would happen when he came back and found out about me. I could see him busting in one day, lighting the torch and taking my body parts off one by one. Other days I saw myself cunning like Odysseus and slipping by him, taking his wife with me. Hedwig and I would settle down somewhere near calm blue water and make beautiful babies.

————

One day, Hedwig came home in the middle of the day. I heard her tires peel and the garage door open and I felt panicked. Their records were all on the floor. I'd been going through them, thinking about the stages in their life together. I liked his taste; all the choices seemed so specific. I yelled "Hello," but she didn't respond. When I got to the adult living room, she was pouring a whiskey at the bar. The sun reflected brightly off the slick tile. John installed them himself, she had told me proudly. I sat on the couch. I asked her to sit down, to talk with me, but she kept shaking her head 'no.' I got up, led her to the recliner, eased her down, and sat on the armrest. She took a drink, rested it back on her knee, and cried. I patted her back, and she pressed her face against my arm, and the back of her head shook against it.

"Is it John?" I asked and she cried harder.

The room was quiet, except for her breathing rapidly and mumbling in German. I told her it would be okay and straightened her up. I petted her hair, and she pulled back and stood.

"You've got to leave," she said and headed back towards the bedroom.

"What happened?" I asked, following in my socks.

It was bright in her room, and I hadn't made the bed yet. She was packing my stuff in an army duffel bag. "Oh, what do you think? Car bomb. It was in a truck filled with loose bits." She sat on the bed and let the bag droop on the floor. "Six of them died." She pushed the bag towards me. "Will you please help? His mother is on her way from Murfreesboro."

I put a sweater in the bag. "That'll take time. You need someone here," I said.

"It's over, Colin. You're very decent. Often nice." She pointed to a pair of my shoes in the corner. "You are a beautiful boy." She got up, picked up the shoes, and pushed them to the bottom of the bag. "Within the instant, boy." She threw it into the hall. "Nice. And Fine. Now please leave with your future." She started talking in German, pacing down the hall. The words sounded pretty hateful, so I was packing now too.

———

When I got to Mama's she was sitting on the porch with a blanket around her waist, the green coat on, and had a book on her knee tilted towards the light. She had started smoking.

I got out of the car and walked up. "You're a smoker now?" I asked.

I went over, turned out the light, and sat on the rail; the orange light from the street threw lined shadows on the porch.

"Hello, son." She flicked her cigarette in the yard.

"John's dead, Mama," I said.

She got up and walked towards me, and I scooted down the rail. "Oh, honey." Her book was folded against her chest. She was almost finished with the book about our street.

"Hedwig and I are done." We had to stop talking when a street sweeper came by. It threw up a fog and left a dusty smell in the air. It took up leaves and dirt in devils, and it had a yellow light on top spinning.

Mama kept nodding until it passed.

"I won't ever see her again," I said.

"That's possible."

"They disappear."

"I know," she said.

I sat and leaned my head against the rails looking through, my feet hanging off the first step of the porch. I put my face against her arm, and she said the air was getting cold. Her arm was across my chest, and I blew warm air into her hand. I kept swallowing, trying not to cry. A lizard crawled along the edge of the ceiling. It had turned to a pale shade of tan and looked panicked in the cold. Mama started humming, and I recognized the tune. It was about monkeys in trees. Lynn and me used to jump around, beating our chests, saying the words. When she stopped, it seemed like the whole town had gone quiet. I closed my eyes hard so that there were points of light floating behind my lids.

"You're very tense, son. Dr. Misty said I should learn to relax my face. Think of all the muscles melting. Like a painting in the sun. Sagging and bleeding away. Start with the top of your head. You have muscles up there too. Your forehead. We are always crunched up, like we are waiting on the next blow. It makes it easier for our muscles to snap when we crunch them up. And so we let them bleed, right off the page. All the way to the bottom ..."

As she spoke I could feel them loosening, even ones I didn't know were there. My nose and jaw. Sometimes we can just go slack and stupid. And then behind my eyes I could see my future that had plenty of options. And that I was only on the side of this trouble, and it was Hedwig in the teeth of it. That eventually she would have to try to go to sleep that night with the mountains of new thought.

# Horses and Tea

Three months after his dad's funeral, Allen wandered, a little lost, through the stalls at the Shelby County equestrian show until he found his uncle Glen's logo. Glen was not really his uncle but had been his dad's best friend. For years, Glen had always been around their house, out in the Tennessee sticks, showing Allen's dad, Big Jim, how to take care of his horse, teaching Allen how to camp, what to do with the cottonmouths that came too close to the camp. Allen could see Glen through the wide slats of the stall, his broad back turned away, his face zeroed in on the horse he was grooming, the brush sweeping away old dirt in a steady shuffle. That's what Glen did, horses. Now, though, Glen was probably always with Allen's mother, walking around his dad's house, grabbing a quick shower, and the bed. Lately, Allen couldn't help these kinds of thoughts. Like people do, Allen used to avoid the thought of his parents having sex . . . but looking at Glen, his father's convenient replacement, Allen could not pretend, could not imagine it any other way than the way it must've been: Glen and his mother had sex, repeated, nightly sex, telling each other, even as his dad was in the next room, his feet properly elevated above his heart, "Oh baby, together at last."

Allen knocked at the gate to the stall, and Glen still brushed the horse in long solid strokes. Only Glen's eyes flicked Allen's way. "Where you been?"

Allen walked into the stall, a little bent over as always from an old injury. He petted the horse, which lurched. It was a tall, dark mare. There was barely room for it in there. Allen brought back his hand, and then checked it to see if his fingers were still there. His back hit the slats when he moved out of room. "Nice horse," Allen said.

"You haven't been out to see your mother in a while. We heard you're about to start teaching up at the high school." Glen opened the horse's mouth, his thumbs raising its lip in an economical movement. Allen's dad died a few weeks before Allen graduated college and had been in the hospital a lot. Unlike his mother, Allen had been loyal. He turned down a chance to study acting in New York and instead went to the University of Memphis not far from his dad's room. His dad would've approved of Allen's graduating. They used to talk about it over games of chess in the hospital. Allen had bought a magnetic board that held the pieces on the board despite the uneven surface of his father's blanketed legs. Allen had become a drama teacher before he even knew it, following a kind of practical course and sticking with his dad.

"Don't you want to slow down, my boy," Big Jim had said. He was a believer in making sure you did something for a living that you liked. "It might be good to move away for awhile. Check the temperature of the water before you jump in, you know what I mean."

Allen never admitted to his dad that the illness was the reason he stayed. So he was about to start teaching *Othello* to sixteen-year-olds. Big Jim hadn't been able to make it to the graduation, and Allen finally did leave right after, lived the whole summer with his now fiancé, Misty, which was why he was here.

"Yep, we start soon. How is Mother?" He looked close for a change in Glen's expression. "You two still … in touch?" The horse backed up again, and Allen moved over; the air felt more open at the gate.

"You still got that little hitch in your step."

On one of their camping trips in the backcountry, Allen had been thrown from his horse, and Glen had gotten the doctor out there very quickly, must've run his own horse ragged. Still, though, they'd been long hard hours on Allen and he'd never quite gotten better. "Ain't it something? I still walk funny. This here is structural damage."

"Thought I'd ask anyway."

"Did you know, Glen, that Genghis Khan died from falling from his horse."

"That right?"

"William the Conqueror too."

Glen looked at him, a little amused. "I guess I better be careful then." Glen stopped smiling. "We wanted to talk to you, Allen. You disappeared after the funeral."

Allen's dad died of colon cancer. His dad had said, "Sometimes medicine loses," after the second remission, the third round of treatment. The third round was when Allen had learned that his mother and Glen had gotten together. Then, as now, it'd been hard for Allen to understand, to do anything around his mother and Glen. In a hospital, Allen had thought, there are a thousand poisons to put in Glen's tea. Some secret dram, a killer flower from Shakespeare days. His dad would tell him to see big pictures, things Misty also told him too now, as he'd gotten

44

ready tonight. And there, looking at Glen's goofy hat, he tried to recite their advice to himself over and over in a quick, wordless hum like meditation. Still, though, the thought of taking the riding crop to Glen's face ... the thought still had a lot of authority.

Allen shook his head and wasn't sure exactly why he was there. "I want to talk to Mother too. To both of you. I'm engaged, Uncle Glen."

"I'll be." Glen picked up the brush and moved it carefully around the mare's eyes. He freed his right hand and extended it to shake, but Allen just folded his arms. He shook his head, amused again, and started brushing. "We know her?"

"You stable her horse. Misty Guffan."

Glen stopped and smiled. "She's a hell of a gal. She didn't mention you."

"I asked her not to. It's an amazing thing, loyalty." Allen could hear his voice projecting out like he was on stage. He took a breath. "Me and Misty get along well. Real comfortable. Going to get married down in Mexico."

Glen nodded from the other side. Allen could see his neck, chin, and the top of his hat. Glen said, "So far away?"

"No families. Her dad is stationed in Germany right now, anyway. I'll come by later in the week and tell Mother," Allen said.

"Misty seems nice, Allen." After a moment Glen grimaced. "We've wanted you to come by. Allen, your mother asked me to move out there for a while."

Allen sat on a low stool.

"For as long as I want," Glen said.

45

They had not talked for some minutes; Glen kept brushing. Allen guessed the mare would be part of the equestrian show. Glen did this for some clients who used his stables. Misty was grooming her own horse down the way. Allen picked up a strand of straw and ran the hard end under the quick of his fingernail.

"How could y'all do that to him?" Allen said.

"We loved him too, you know." Glen drew the brush against his jeans and loose hair fell to the dirt. "I guess we feel like you and Misty do."

Allen grabbed a new piece of straw and tucked it in his cheek. "I liked it better when y'all were sneaking around. Misty said you're making all sort of improvements on Dad's land."

Glen exhaled through clenched teeth. The brush kept its pace, and his eyes were dull. "Your dad bought good land cheap but he was just the weekend type." It was true. Big Jim was never more than half interested in ranches. He just never wanted to forget how he grew up.

Allen wondered how his mother could choose Glen, a man who could devote himself to horses with that blank mind. Allen's father had been an imaginative man and taught college for twenty-five years. Big Jim had been sharp, but he'd always been the same kind of country kid. Some of the students and other professors thought he was a bit quaint the way he would scoop up persimmons right off the ground under a campus tree and eat them. That was where his father met Glen. Glen was a student in Big Jim's class, and during a one-on-one conference, he had asked Glen straight out if he really wanted to be in college. Glen said he wanted to rope calves, and Allen's dad had said something like, "If you're waiting for permission, you've got it." Big Jim said one time that Glen had a toughness that other people lacked. Big Jim told Allen once, "He's the kind this country doesn't make enough of these days." As a young kid and a teenager, Allen had bought it all too. Followed Glen around the pasture every day. That is, until the accident. Even after, though, Glen had been good to him, taught him how to whittle the shapes of animals into soft wood, got Allen his own knife made of real bone. And that was how it was for a while, Big Jim teaching him chess and Glen teaching him about the outdoors, and now he had none of it.

Allen stood and held out the straw so Glen would have to look at it. "I swear. When are you going to look at yourself, Glen? Your rodeo days are over, you know." Allen threw down the straw, and walked to the end of the stall. The wood had been freshly painted, but all he could smell was horse and straw. Glen eventually made it as a bull rider on the circuit but broke and popped out his shoulder too many times. He kept horses now for other people— followed them around with a shovel as far as Allen could tell. Now, just about anything could knock Glen's shoulder out or cause pain—hammering, hauling fence, opening a stuck laundry door.

"Take care, hotshot." Glen finally looked up from the horse and looked back. "You can't be mad at us forever."

Allen walked toward the gate. He turned and looked at Glen. "How insensitive of me to grieve for a few months."

"I've got to get this horse ready, but you should

47

know we talked to your father about it before he died."

Allen waved his hand in the air. "Good luck with your little chores there."

————

Allen sat in the corner of the stands to see the equestrian riders and Misty coming towards him for at least half the lap and then to see her from behind the other half, her back straight and trim, her long boots and tight pants. He thought of his father in one room dying, and his mother and Glen somewhere else, humping. How had that transition been so easy for her, where she could say Glen's name instead of his father's and could push Glen down on a bed, throw his hat across the room, bite his neck, rip the buttons on his shirt, one of those loud obnoxious western shirts? Easy to unsnap buttons, like a call girl's panties. She could lie there after and run her hand across his chest and laugh. They were probably there in the hospital searching for an empty bed while the old man was trying to hang on.

The event started and a pretty blonde girl circled the stadium four times. She touched the horse's neck while making a turn, and it slowed its pace, but Allen didn't understand the event even though Misty had described it. It would be the first time he'd seen Misty ride in full-on competition.

There in the beginning with Misty, Allen's life had been a whirlwind, or like two sides of a coin from some country he'd never heard of. For part of the day, he'd be with his father, watching some history channel special on land mines, some GI emptying a whole sack of them out of a helicopter, into the jungle, his father making some comment about the General Electric Corporation. Then, leaving, feeling a bit washed off in fresh air, he'd go over to Misty's, where he felt even lighter, more like what he was, a young guy with everything before him. With Misty, the things they said and did, did not stay. Their great meaning would float away, as soon as it was out in the present. The words on the Scrabble board would be reshuffled in the pouch, or just put away, or the meals that they would try to make from some far-off culture would get eaten, the smells drifting out the window.

"Don't worry," Misty would say. "Yams are the same thing as a sweet potato."

"Yam stands for manliness in Nigeria ... It is the king of crops. I read that in a play once. Maybe I should double up on them."

"Maybe I'll let you have my skin. I like how you do that," she would say, looking up at him. "Talk about people in books as if they're real. Like they live down the street."

"After the fall, I was stuck in a bed for a very long time," he'd said, wrapping the yam in foil.

"You should try to ride again," Misty had suggested. "I could teach you right this time. And we could ride, and we could make silly jokes about the history of the sidesaddle."

"One word. Christopher Reeve. Freaking Superman. Horses, gravity, they don't care about people."

"Okay. But that was more than one word."

Allen looked at the arena. The decorations altered from the last time he'd been there. Although these equestrian sports were held in the same building that Allen used to watch Glen rope in, Misty's events were nothing like rodeos.

He asked the woman next to him how they kept score. Misty had told him when they first started dating, but her explanation had been technical. The woman's hair was fake red and thinning and looked nice with her blue jumpsuit.

"The riders have to show control and *harmony* with their horse. It's not like the jumping sports, not about power. *Grace* and control. Just watch the horse," she said and bounced her hand up and down in the air, as if a conductor. "If the horse knows what to do without being told, it means it knows its rider well, hours of training."

Allen told her thanks and watched a few riders, trying to understand the way she said "harmony" and "grace." As he was ready to say it was cheesy, he saw Misty. It wasn't only that she looked good in the white pants; it wasn't that she was both young and more worldly than him; she was excellent at it. Allen got a surge when she went by him. The stuffy breeze, the footfalls like a silent movie. The clay artfully shot out from under the hooves.

The woman next to him touched his arm, pointed to Misty and said, "*That* is how it's done."

And he got numb all over and asked the woman to see her program. "Misty Guffan," he said.

"Oh yes, she is good—barely lost in last year's collegiate circuit."

"She will be my wife."

———

Allen and his mother were in a sunroom his dad had added many years ago, and the sun came through the floor-to-ceiling glass door. She used it as a sitting room: concrete floors, tall plants along the windows, and iron furniture with teal, floral cushions. Dust drifted through the light in little strings. It always surprised him to see that air was filled up that way. It had been the room he would practice scenes in when he'd been in high school, and she would read the other parts and encourage him, help him learn the words and dances.

His mother was moving teddy bears from one corner to the other, neglecting her tea. She dressed up bears as a hobby. "I'm glad you are here. You can help me move a tree in from the truck." She grabbed a cheerleader bear with an orange "V" on it and put it at the front of the display she was making to take to the flea market. It would sell because the Vols had won the national championship that year. When the big flea market rolled around, she would load up all the bears and sell.

"Uncle Glen can help you. He's strong." Allen took a sip. She made great tea. His father always bragged about it, and his dad would make fun of Allen when he'd drink a Coke in the mornings.

She sat and leaned forward, looking down at the glass table, and brushed some hair behind her ear. It would've been gray if she let it, and it was thick and wavy. She bent and drew the edge of her dress across the glass table. The fingerprints disappeared.

Allen wondered if Glen liked her in dresses, if he would raise them slowly and kiss the new inches of her thighs. Allen's face was warm.

51

"The three of us were always friends. Your dad had so many friends. I was his best one. Then one day he is gone—there was just nothing anybody could do." She rubbed her forehead.

Allen stood and turned on the ceiling fan. The wall was brick like the outside of the house. It had been where they used to open Christmas presents. He put his hand against the brick; the fan spun. Its fake gold engraving did not look as fancy as he once thought it. He saw that she was about to speak, so he said, "The least you could do is get married." He sat and drew his cup up smoothly.

"No. I was married to your father, for one thing. And Glen and I are something different. He's younger, and we expect different things from each other. I'm keeping this place in my name. He's just using it, adding onto the stable part. We think it's the way to do it," she said.

"Since when are mothers so cynical?" he asked.

She patted him on the knee and stood. "This way, you'll get all the money when I'm dead."

"Well, I'm getting married. Next week we leave for Mexico."

She sat and looked worried. Allen shifted on the couch. The edges of the teal cushions were hard where they met the iron framing. Iron furniture, in Allen's opinion, was a bad idea. He shook his head. "I'm sorry that you're not coming. I am going to get married, though. I love her, Mother. Be happy for me."

"It's just surprising. When Glen let it slip, I was just surprised." She hugged him. She said she was excited and asked who and when and where. Allen told her they'd get married in Cabo. He told her a brief version of his and

52

Misty's time together.

She said, "You never do talk to me. I had no idea. Can you try, dear, to change that?"

"So you're happy then?" Allen asked, and she nodded. "You're happy about me and Misty, I mean," he said.

———————

Allen and Misty were in the Pacific Ocean. A Skimmer flew by and scooped a fish not too far from them, and Allen told her it was one of the few birds whose lower jaw was longer than its upper.

"Like a shovel," she said, and Allen kissed her. The reflection in her glasses showed the Cabo beach crowd, and she pressed herself close to him, and a wave came up and made them tumble. The Pacific waves were tougher than the ones in the Gulf. With a salty mouth, the muted waves in his ears, he laughed and it stung. She spit, and he put his arms back around her, and she rubbed her hips against him, and he got hard.

Allen looked at the beach again, but nobody watched them. It was just water and the flat blue sky around with a tiny shrimper way out.

"They're catching our dinner," he said.

"Hunger means you want something else," she said.

They were drifting out and let their bodies float loose. He rubbed her thigh, and it was grainy.

"Now what kind of husband will you be?" she asked and ducked her hair back into the water. She lay back and floated, and Allen put his left arm under her back like a magician. Half of her head was under water and she said, "You will have two wives in Provo that I never hear from. You will wake one morning to find a note that says, 'Gone to France.' We will be old and dance in our house shoes." She smiled. "You will be so loving that I will despise you—you tiptoer, you coffee-bringer. You will ignore me in the evenings 'to do your reading.' You will be wildly jealous and stalk me from bushes. You will beat me on occasion and I won't leave you."

He brought her ears out of the water and said, "Oh, no, no, no. And the other, *who* would seduce *you*?"

She smiled and said, "Jealousy then. You watch my eyes, my eyes admire a European bathing suit."

"I noticed you noticed the cabana boy." He dropped his arm and she went under smoothly. She moved as confidently in the water as she did on a horse. She carried herself that way, and he wondered if she ever got caught off guard.

She swam towards the shore, and he followed. When they could put their feet down, she kept backing away until he tackled her, and she bit his ear.

She pointed out towards the horizon—it was blue and smoky, and besides the shrimper, gliding slowly, like a hearse, he didn't see any living thing. She said, "Cabo beaches have riptide. Some people get caught and get sucked away."

"I would let you stand on my shoulders," he said. They were getting closer to the beach, and he carried her in his arms.

"One of us should survive," she said, and he set her

down when she got heavy. She walked in the knee-high water, and he stayed half- submerged, sitting on the bottom. A swell came up that drifted him closer.

"Come on," she said.

"I need to stay in for a second. Calm my married instrument."

"You need to do something else with that." She went towards their chairs and turned, walking backwards with a promising look. As she was toweling off, he hoped that he had what it took to keep her happy. When she had phoned her dad after the ceremony, she had told him that she and Allen would be great together and that Allen was smart and funny.

Allen wondered what adjectives she used for him in her mind when he wasn't there, and he had the admittedly small wish that they were that he was attractive and wonderful in bed. Before Misty his relationships worked poorly. The only other long-term girlfriend was a tennis player named Nina, and that had been a failure by his count. He saw her at a restaurant with some other guy, but that was not the worst thing about that night. What bothered him was his own reaction. He froze in the bar and stared at her from behind a wooden column, the way she leaned into his conversation, the way she buttered her roll in a way that made it clear that Nina was sleeping with the guy. And he just left. He didn't even confront her. A glass of water spilled in her lap, at the very least, was required, a demand for satisfaction from the usurping dog of a boy, something.

When Misty and he got back to the room, they had sex while the shrimp were boiling. She said she enjoyed it, and he said he'd try not to be so quick later. She had bought a camping stove at the Walmart super-mercado, hoping to save a little money, and they ate on the balcony. They peeled shrimp in deliberate motions and competed —who could do it without breaking the shells into pieces. They dropped the shells from the fifth story, and when a guy from the second floor stuck his head out, they laughed and backed up against the stucco wall. They'd been making fun of the other tourists who never left what she'd started calling the compound. She smiled like she did when she was being clever, folding her upper lip against her gum. Allen faked a throwing motion, and she opened her mouth, and he tossed a shrimp in.

They leaned on the rail, and she rested her arm against his back.

She pointed to the ridge down the beach from the hotel and said, "Mick Jagger lives there."

"Is that the kind of guy you want?" he asked. Now there was a guy who never made the safe, dutiful choice.

"We should go hear a band tonight."

He asked, "You think we'll be happy?"

"I'm just in this for the honeymoon."

"When Jefferson wrote the Declaration, he changed 'pursuit of property' to 'pursuit of happiness.' I was in a play about him and John Adams."

"An idealistic change," she said.

"He scratched it right out. They were frenemies but made up. Died the same day. July Fourth."

"Allen, I want you to do something for me. I'd like it if we could be around your family a lot when we get back. I like them."

He nudged a loose bit of concrete over the edge.

"You mean Mother and Uncle Glen? That's what you mean by my family."

"It's just been so long since I've been around one."

Her dad, an army medical doctor, had been stationed near Heidelberg since she was sixteen, and she hadn't seen her mother since she was twelve. She grabbed his forearm. "Really, Allen, can't you give them a better chance?"

———

When they got back to Tennessee, Allen made good on the promise and was visiting his mother while Misty was riding. Allen sat on the new screened-in porch Glen had added. He stained it turquoise himself then immediately scored it, so it had that twangy, faux-native look. With a glue gun Allen's mother stuck an ascot on the neck of a grizzly bear's smoking jacket; the gun gave off a strong smell.

"Do you think Uncle Glen would ever cheat on you?"

"He knows about my .38," she said and smiled. She held up the finished bear.

He nodded.

"You used to like Glen. Beg to go camping with *Uncle Glen*. 'Oh, Mama, he doesn't even use a tent.'"

He nodded and started reading the sophomore textbook again. He was having trouble even getting to the good parts of *As You Like It*. The students were having trouble getting past cross-dressing jokes. He imagined do-

ing something more contemporary and performing himself
again. Occasionally the class would be on track and he
would read the part and feel the class listening, the emotion glazed on the words, and he could feel that he still had
it. He would go home and flip through the arts section and
see that even the Memphis companies were about ten years
behind.

Looking at his watch, he calculated how long Misty
and Glen had been riding. Every day after he taught school,
he would come over to Glen's ranch and wait until Misty
was done training and giving lessons to older, wealthier
women, the people that kept the stable thing going. Glen
had saved all his winnings from the pro circuit and put a lot
of money and work into Big Jim's place, what Jim called
his pasture. There was plenty of space for Misty to keep her
horse and give lessons.

The thick, wooden rails on the porch looked like a
blind man carved them. Glen had two high-tech office
chairs. One of those mesh jobs that must have cost a
thousand bucks and didn't fit in with the western decor,
but when you sat, you felt like every muscle was supported,
that the manufacturers had your body in mind. Glen
claimed to have Allen's bad back in mind when he bought
the chairs.

"They sure do spend a lot of time together," Allen
said.

"Who?" his mother asked. She wound the electric
cord around the gun and put it in a box.

"Uncle Glen and Misty."

"They like the same things." She stood to go in and
stopped. "Whatever you're thinking, stop. Strange thought.

That they might be ..." She shook her head. "You're so strange."

"She rides arenas in competition. Why does she practice every day in open space? How would that open space benefit the horse?"

"She likes to ride, Allen." She went inside, holding the bear in front of her.

It was a wonderful chair. Here, Allen could watch Misty. The sun was going down, and the pasture was quiet; the gnats caught the light.

"Don't those look nice," said Allen, and then he realized he was alone. The bugs made dots of gold, flecks chasing each other and folding back to where they'd come from, some secret chore finished. They reminded him today he should try to notice the way Misty's hair looked in sunlight—wild, out of place. They'd ride up, her hair all free, then she would smile at something Glen had said. Allen figured he'd see the two of them any moment. What could Glen possibly have to say to her? Those dull eyes, that silly hat, that insufferable relaxed composure. A light touch on her wrist, perhaps. Next time pushing her hair behind her ear. I know a quiet place—a brook—where we can sit and rest awhile.

He saw them. They rode up the incline towards the stable, and Allen looked at his watch—ninety minutes. He said, "Did you all have fun?"

They didn't hear him. She trotted the horse up the gravel drive, stiff legged in the stirrups. He stood and asked his question again.

The screen was between them, and in the shadows, her face looked tired, or maybe even red-faced from

59

exertion. She got off the horse and loosened the bridle. "Glen thinks it will be a bad year for wheat."

"Does he? Such talents," Allen said and opened the door and stood on the steps.

Glen was walking up from the stables. Two dogs were humping in the gravel. Glen picked up a rock and threw it at them. "Have you no shame?"

Misty laughed and patted her horse Roger.

"Hell, he's even got a sense of humor," Allen said.

She looked at him. "Were your students bad in class today or something?"

"Yeah," he said, and she put her hand on his shoulder. He could smell her sweat. "I thought I'd grill some lamb chops tonight."

"Fine." She pinched his arm and led her horse toward the stable. She talked to her horse: "Lamb, Roger, not horse, not tonight." She called to Glen to wait up.

———

Allen and Misty sat in their living room; it was theirs now. They had bought it instead of renting. When picking it out, he quoted a line from Joyce he had underlined. "Landlord never dies, they say. Other steps into his shoes when he gets his notice to quit."

Each had a glass of wine balanced on a knee as they listened to a variety show on the radio. Someone was playing piano, and a woman was talking like a Chicago gangster moll.

The show ended and Misty said, "Your mother is

lucky to have Uncle Glen."

"For Christ's sake, haven't we had enough of them for this week?" Allen got up, set his wine on the stereo and turned off the power.

"He's a good, hardworking man, I—"

"I said shut up."

She stood and said, "Give it a rest, Allen. She loves Glen now."

Allen slapped her. Hit her right above the ear. She dropped her glass. With her mouth opened, she looked at him, to the broken wineglass, to him, and kicked him between the legs.

He fell back hard against the wall. He couldn't catch his breath. Bending over, his face two inches from the hardwood, he kept sucking in.

She put her hand on the back of his head.

His long breaths weren't getting any better.

Pausing to look at him while putting on her coat, she asked, "You need a doctor?" She started for the phone. "Or maybe I should call the fucking cops."

"Wait."

She put the phone to her ear.

"Look," Allen said and leaned back against the wall, his knees bent in front of him. "I am fine. Not so fragile."

She took a Kleenex from her pocket and picked up the broken stem.

"Leave it," he said.

She picked up another large piece. "Psycho."

"I'm sorry," he said, and then asked, "Are you screwing Uncle Glen?"

She sat on the sofa, the bits of glass in her hands

next to her car keys. In a calm voice, as calm as he'd ever heard anyone curse, she said, "You're fucking ridiculous, Allen."

"Yes or no?"

"No, Allen." She stood and walked toward the kitchen. When she passed him, she said lowly, "What a dick."

He heard her throw the glass away and close a door. While she was gone, he did a quick evaluation of what had happened and knew she was right but didn't know what to do about it. He bet his father had never been such an ass. The couch had a stain on the leg now, like a tattoo. She was probably right. That Glen and his mother seemed happy.

———————

Allen woke up when Misty got back. He was still on the floor slumped against the wall and the stereo.

"You're back," he said and rubbed his face.

She stood looking over him. She still had her coat on. "Tell me why I should be."

He looked down at his hands. "It's me. Being made a fool of. I just ... "

"You could give me some credit. Have a little self-respect."

"Yes. I'll do it all. It's all my bad." He started to get up but thought it might be interpreted as aggression.

She bent her knees and was staring right at him. "I wonder if you can, Allen."

She pivoted and went down the hall, and he heard her climb the stairs. He exhaled and went to the sofa and lay back, adjusting the pillow against the armrest before he turned out the light. His pants were almost dry from where the wine splattered.

So he wasn't in their little riding club. So Tennessee could look real pretty on the back country hills, where you sit in the shade of this tree—finally the relief of it—a short, spread-out tree, where you tie up the horse and lie during the right time of year, a bit of cheese, some deer jerky Glen made himself. So they'd always have these secret moments. It wasn't even a real ranch, not like Glen claimed, Allen thought. Then Allen shook his head and laughed at himself, and it sounded scary in the room.

He closed his eyes and tried to imagine himself as a different man, one that could walk around confidently with Misty, accepting the space between them, appreciating his own secret knowledge of her. That she was the only thing he had going for him. It'd been easy to just wrap himself up in what happened to his dad and not have to deal with anything else.

He thought of his mother, the image of her as she was at the hospital, her reddish hair brushed back, the champagne streaks of gray. Her voice deep and reassuring in his father's ear. Her energy, the lively movements of her long dresses as she went about the room, the kind words she had for both Allen and his father. The cool touch of her gold necklace against his face. Her skin still young and cool. He tried to imagine her as someone that he didn't know. As just a woman, a lively one with plenty of fire left, even underneath her clothes. A person able to evolve

63

honorably along with things in her life. He opened his eyes, and thought, this is the woman that Glen knows.

Allen stood, his head throbbing again on the sides, his vision blurry from the rush of blood. He thought he heard someone calling out for him and he walked ahead, feeling along the walls of the hallway. He put his hand on the staircase and looked up into the darkness, waiting to hear his name again, some invitation to come back to the room.

# Back to Zero

After several years together, I was surprised that Diane was still so interested in counting the freckles on my chest. She took off my glasses and smoothed my eyebrows down. I'd always wanted to grow those big Oppenheimer brows that reach out like insects. They probably gave him some extra information. I bet he knew when it would rain before the rest of us did.

"You need to pluck more," she said. She got some tweezers from her bag and inspected.

"I want to look wise." She yanked a group. "Ouch. I don't like to do things that hurt, Diane."

"Sure you do." We'd just been biting each other's thighs, finding that edge just before you say quit. "You do everything half-ass." She took three more. Like a lot of our friends, Diane put up the poster of Albert Einstein sticking out his tongue. I thought people should put Oppenheimer up there, that physics ain't about fun, that there is a moment of fear when we look at the reality we shape and say, the horror, I am become death.

I sucked in through clenched teeth. Diane was good with the tweezers and had this physical confidence. She took care of people going into and out of heart surgery. Was there in the room handing things to the doctor and suctioning things when they drained the blood to work on the heart. The key is to keep them cold enough, induce this hibernation. A doctor in Chicago, Daniel Hale Williams, did one of the first successful heart sew ups. He was one of the few black doctors who'd managed to get surgical training and a place to work. He fixed a guy who was stabbed in the heart. The guy all bleeding, Williams must have been willing to try anything, and two months later the knife guy was just walking around like the rest of us.

Diane was around those kind of emergencies and quick thinking. Whenever she told stories about her job, I would think about Diane and grownup people and how I was glad there were capable people in this world. I was starting to choose who would be my family. My real family had done such a crappy job of it that I'd only kept a brother around, and now there was Diane too and Guy. It would be a meritocracy, very hard to enter like heaven and the needle eye. When I told my friends I'd divorced my family, I made it sound humorous, like the *Goodfellas'* scene, "No, you see. Here's how it's going to be. I divorce *you*. You got that, clown."

I would sometimes convince myself that Diane would stick in the family. So even though my eyebrows were hurting, I said, "The world needs people like you, Di."

"You usually forget that I am a force of good in your life," she said and kissed me between the eyes. She had on nice-smelling lotion. "I feel like we can be loud this morning." My roommate Guy did not come home after his show last night. He had probably hooked up with some girl who liked his singing and his carefully torn jeans.

Diane took out a small pair of scissors and opened and closed them in a threatening way. "Nose hair."

I shimmied out of bed. She walked towards me on her knees and clipped the air. She had on a long blue sleep shirt that accentuated the curve of her hips—once I had measured its angle in relation to her navel for my last paper in college: "The Geometry of Attraction."

I threw a blanket over her and tucked the edges up under her, so she couldn't move, and stayed there with her. When the laughter died out, we just lay there for a few minutes and she said that my feet were cold.

———

After Diane left, I drove to work late, the weird commute through a tough section of Memphis. No one cared when I got there as long as it was before the meetings. I had been doing figures at the chemical plant for three years now, seeing Diane all the while. They'd put all the factory-type polluters on Florida Street near the poorest neighborhoods. You'd think there'd be a palm tree here and there, a nod to vacation, but it was just a string of warehouses then small houses without air conditioning, the people out in the yard under the trees, sitting on plastic furniture. When I first would drive past them, I'd wave to them like my dad used to do when we were out on the country roads where we lived. Here, no one waved back. I didn't even live there. But I'd have these flashes that I should. I'd pass the community center and think: I should volunteer one day and give math classes. Make it fun. Show the calculations that happen in the beats of pop music, or the geometry in Jordan's triangle offense. I never actually stopped though.

Like most whites, I'd grown up out east. They tried to set up the interstate so that people would never need to come into this neighborhood in between downtown and out east. It towered over the neighborhood, as if on stilts, like it didn't want to sink into an icky bog.

They'd built the overpass closest to work too short. Moving vans and delivery trucks were always slamming into it. I saw one wedged under there on the way to work one day, and I looked it up online. Someone had posted a funny YouTube about it. Footage of about thirty trucks running into it. I didn't want to laugh at first, but then it just kept happening, and I'd watched it carefully even though I knew what was coming. And I watched with Diane. And then with Guy. And then at work sometimes when I got bored. When I should have been planning to build a house with Diane to keep up with this timetable she had in her mind. Even though we were only twenty-five, she wanted to build out in Eads where there was still plenty of land.

I'd tried to personalize my section of work, using the Photoshop at work to do my own posters, not unlike the ones I saw Guy make for his shows. Oppenheimer saying, "I need physics more than friends," his arm around a cropped image of Marilyn Monroe. We needed a presentation of particle flow in 3-D models. I added psychedelic colors Guy would have liked and the slides were looking like a Jefferson Airplane-type poster. That's when Diane called.

She was ready for me to commit to buying some land just off I-40. Her schedule was usually three twelve-hour shifts in a week and then four days off, so I would get the calls on the days off.

"Four Oaks in the back."

"The back of what?" I asked. In the particle flow model the particles were coupling in the conditions I was simulating. Coupling naturally flowing to areas of closest need. Clustering. The birth of little families. It was natural for Diane and I to have this whole house thing. It would be space for me to build the new family.

"The house, silly," she said. "The back porch. There are three sweet gums too. Think of the falls we'll have. The whip-poor-wills in the spring."

"I'll swing by after work, babe. But listen, I am swamped here." She apologized, since I was saying it gruffly. I was annoyed that my fall and all my future falls were being planned for me, a fine life. I closed my eyes and tried to breathe slowly. I read somewhere that people breathed too much. In my head, I could see my parents who should have divorced about ten years before they did. When you start the simulation with screams and shaking walls and wake up to see the little doorjam to your mother's bedroom torn away, the unpainted inner wood out and new looking, when you start the model there, it never seemed to advance much.

I opened my eyes feeling a calmer breathing pattern. The colors on the graph were starting to snap visually, and I was half wishing that it were an actual creation I was doing, an art project, rather than a part of a presentation, and I spent the rest of the day finishing it out.

After work, instead of driving out to Eads, I went to the city park near the zoo and watched people play Frisbee and caught up on episodes with HBO GO on my phone. I could hear a monkey in the distance, a gibbon. I used to like to go watch them. Once when my parents took me to the zoo, they started arguing in the snake house and my mother walked off and my father muttered after her, following but refusing to walk faster in order to catch up. I managed to slip back into a darker corner by the bats, seeing them whizzing by, my shirt purple in the black light. I saw my parents circle the exhibits a few times, calling my name. It felt powerful to see them at the same purpose, only when they left the house thinking I'd gone outside, I really did feel lost.

This chapter of my life was supposed to be self-authored, but I still wasn't sure where I was. I didn't even want to need physics the way Oppenheimer did. Diane was ready for a family, a kind of good individual square of the world, which made sense for her, but I felt like I had nothing to add there. Guy needed music.

This playing keep up with two people, Diane and Guy. Guy the dude everyone loved that managed to lovingly break all the rules. Guy who never settled. He had not forgotten what being young could be, such constant motion, that somehow a person could just keep moving forward without ever running out and resting.

I finally drove home but Diane had not showed up yet, so my whole fictional outing was a joke. Guy was in the house we rented, with a digital sixteen-track on the piano bench, the levels going up and down on the screen. He kicked at a chair close to the machine. "I need you on back-up," he said.

"I've got that LOFT problem, remember," I said. He'd always say that about other musicians: lack of fucking talent.

"This is a Neil Young thing." He lit a cigarette. I hadn't yet convinced him to smoke outside. "Whatever you got will do."

We recorded for a while. Although I got bored, it was nice in the end. To have a product. To see the volume levels go up and down; thirty seconds of history, digitized as it was. I was still impressed that you could email someone a song, that all these matters of significance were objectless. I understood the algorithm of it. But sometimes I still feel impressed, like an old man saying, 'You can do what?'

The section got a thumbs-up from him when it was finished, and feeling like we had earned it, we poured our beer in a glass like real adults. He'd found a case of TGI Fridays' glasses at a vintage shop from when it was a cool place where Big Star and Billy Joel used to hang out. He'd been shopping at their record section too. He'd also found an old 78 of Big Boy Crudup doing "That's All Right Mama."

"I wonder how many millions Elvis made on this guy's song," I asked.

"That's Memphis for you. Our school has the top-notch drama program, and the one down the street doesn't have air conditioning. I read this Crudup guy had to go back to farming instead of music."

"All this equipment you have and the good reviews. I just wish guys like him would have had more press and stuff."

"The Sullivan Show would've been nice, but he would've had to sing to that stupid dog. No, the only thing this guy needed to make it big was to be white."

My glass was halfway to my mouth and I stopped. It was such a simple, true statement. I never thought much about privilege, the thousand moments like this where one life is easier than another one, where obstacles are got around, a person just keeps their push going down one hill and up the other. I had the sudden fear that it had made me stupid and that if the choices in your life were too easy then you can't understand them and you're just eating up space that another person might be enjoying.

———————

When Diane came over later that night, she asked me if I wanted to move in to her place instead of waiting for us to plan and build our own place, and I said I'd think about it, and that didn't go over well. The conversation had started off fine. We'd been remembering how much fun it had been when we sanded and painted some of her old furniture. There'd been a mouse that came out in the middle of it, darting across the floor like a shadow or the light from a passing car. She lived out east in this aluminum can townhouse in Germantown. So all of a sudden it was just this memory of the mouse, and then I was supposed to live with her right away.

She lay on the floor with all the pillows and blankets. The mattress was oddly flat with just the sheet: the white line looked like a close horizon.

She hadn't spoken to me since she had made the pallet. She pressed mute on the TV, and I sat up. Round two.

She moved bits of dust from the floor together. She cut her eyes to me. "Chicken shit."

"Maybe I don't deserve you," I said.

"You deserve your 'maybes,'" she said. "You can write to me in ten years and report what your chicken shit 'maybe' gets you."

There was rustling and voices in the hallway, and I heard Guy talking to his latest girlfriend. I said, "He'll want us to say hello to this new girl."

"You cannot allow yourself to be in this moment. Don't you feel *anything* for me?"

She was about to start with the self-pity, a tactic that always had me helpless. "Diane, there's something I ought to tell you about New Year's."

"Another hall of fame moment," she said.

We had gotten in a real tangle that night. I went to Guy's big show in LA, and we stayed at my brother Don's. Don dealt with our family by moving seventeen hundred miles away. My brother got Guy the show, but only six people showed up, all Don's friends, each friend coupled up, except a girl named Julia who sat next to me and thought I was clever.

Diane kept calling all night, angrier each time that I wasn't with her. During the last call, she said, "You're not even here, so shut the fuck up; I'm going to find someone who is." I'd been trying to tell her that New Year's was a false idea. That given the way the earth rotates it was only a way to sell champagne. After she hung up, I took it for clear that it was over, and spent the night making out in various places with Julia, including her apartment.

Against my wall, Diane started thudding her head through the propped-up pillow. Not hard but enough to create a pulse.

"I'm no saint, Diane," I said.

"Big news," she said and thumped the edge of her glass.

"I slept with another woman."

"Ugh." She held her head still and breathed deep. "Slime." She rearranged the pillows against the wall, and I wondered whether she'd throw the glass at me. She let out some nervous laughs.

"You're laughing?" I asked.

"I've been trying to find the right time for us to move forward. Failure. Years of waiting."

"I would never call it that."

"What do you know? You are small. Micro. Micro Machine." She got up. Her shirt had a few spills on it, but she still looked nice. She had a red scarf on, untied around her neck, and when she passed me, it brushed my leg.

She grabbed a video from the shelf and held it out. She gave the fakest smile. She turned and put the video in and said, "Now I can hate you. Whenever I remember something good, your slime will drive it away." She sat on the floor and pushed play. It was a pornographic movie she got me once when she went to travel nurse in Bristol. She was over there for eight weeks and said I could use the tape. She turned the volume up as loud as it would go. I put my hands over my ears.

She raised her glass and smiled. "Don't miss your

favorite part, Charlie." There were two girls sunbathing on patio furniture. A neighbor was hiding but not very well. They invited him over.

"Do you want me to drive you home?" I asked, still plugging my ears.

She held up her wine as if she'd just won a race. "Later. It's still snowing." She pointed out the window like a bored stewardess.

"When's later."

"Quiet. She's about to remove her panties."

I got up and looked out the window. Orange halos surrounded the streetlights, and the snow looked like flecks of copper floating down slowly like a camera trick in a movie. I knew that in a vacuum everything fell at the same speed, but it was hard to believe in a place with no air.

From the hallway, I heard Guy saying something.

"Will you mute it?" I asked.

She did.

From beyond the door, Guy said, "Um, Charlie. Will you turn your movie down?"

I looked at Diane, and she shook her head. I said, "No, Guy. Not right now."

———————

It stopped snowing around three a.m., and I took Diane home. The streets were slick, so I kept it in the low gears. Traffic had made two strips through the ice, which made the road look long and enduring. An equal sign that would never stop.

"Thanks for driving slow," she said. She used to complain that when we argued in the car, I drove dangerously on purpose.

"I'm not mad at you. It's all me," I said. I slid left against the ice, then straightened up when I hit the worn strip.

"That makes sense." She cupped her hand around her mouth and nose. "Does my breath stink?"

"A little." I leaned over and opened the glove box. "There's a mint in there."

She offered me one, and when she gave it to me I grabbed her hand. She held my hand for a moment. I got the feeling that if either one of us wanted, we could've pulled it together still. If I were more sorry, I could turn things on again like after a power outage. And if she kept staring up and still held on to my hand, I would let it go on still. She wiggled her hand free and put a mint in her mouth.

A streetlight at her corner turned red and I went through it. She turned on the radio and kept switching it from love songs. She left it on a Bob Dylan song about political change.

"I can put on that band you like," I said.

"Quiet." I pulled into her drive and pulled the emergency brake. She had her head against the seat, her eyes closed. She opened the door and cold air came in and blew her hair.

———————

I got back home around four a.m., and Guy was still up recording some piano. He had the top of the piano opened with the mic sticking in as if eager. I tapped him on the shoulder, and he took off the earphones and pushed stop.

"It's through, Diane and I." I sat on the organ bench making chords that didn't sound.

"Damn," he said. "I wasn't sure what that movie meant."

The center C note was missing. Guy said it made chords sound pleasantly off.

"Do you want to get drunk?" he asked.

"Not that. I don't want to go to sleep though."

He got up and a dust ball under the piano swirled. From the window, he said, "We can play in the snow." I said okay even though it seemed like a rude thing to do.

Outside, Guy took running starts and slid on the street trying to keep balance.

"Try it," he said.

I tried and fell hard on my hip. "This sucks."

"Follow me," he said.

Guy and I went to the corner, removed a plastic dumpster lid and slid down the hill in front of our house for a while. The final run bettered them all. We jumped on the lid at the same time and really sailed, bumping up and down, the slush crunching under the lid. We went through the stop sign that time, and I wondered if the momentum might keep. A slope drifted us right, and we smashed into a red Honda and the alarm sounded.

I was on the ground laughing, and Guy was standing up looking at me.

"Are you all right?" He bent and nudged my shoulder.

"All right he says." The cold from the street drifted down my neck, the ice in sharp grooves against my knuckles.

"That laugh is really scary," he said, trying to help me up.

"You'd never guess it'd get this cold."

————

Guy was not there when I came home from work the next day. I sat on his bed and wondered if he had washed his sheets since he and Gina had been together. The mattress was, predictably, on the floor, and his gaudy flyers and art were stapled to the walls. I tried to imagine what his girlfriends thought of him, why they thought this room was so special.

I scooted over to the sixteen track at the end of the bed and turned it on. Maybe his girls would listen in bed. He'd put on a song he made and say, "The girl in this song is you." She'd put her head against his armpit and trace the design on his T-shirt, one he'd printed himself; she would dream, like he had hypnotized her, of a world where songs saved communities and she knew the shaman.

In fact, she would be a lot like Diane, but he'd find some confident way to go about it and never promise too much. And in the end, his girlfriends would leave and were never heard from again, and he never had to add up the things he lost.

78

Even I sometimes felt that around him—like every-thing was possible. He had all these things, gifts, I could never have. There would always be fear and guilt, and a bunch of regret.

On the sixteen track there was a button that read "BTZ." That was where I had gone with Diane, back to zero. The concept of zero had changed math forever. The Europeans didn't have it at first. The Babylonians, the Maya, then the Persians who called it *Sifr*. Now I needed the number that is not anything to program electrolysis for caustic sodas. And yet, if I were not there to make the program, there would be someone else and there would still be paper and paper mills.

I scrolled through his songs. He'd been working on them for most of the year: oboes, clarinets, a bass sax, trumpets, a viola, me in the background banging a castiron skillet, violins, two cellos, a Moog, an elementary class singing verses, washboards, saws, a triangle, the sound of tires on gravel. I scrolled down to my favorite song and pushed play.

He had gotten the Memphis Horns to play on the song. My brother Don had gotten them some movie work that paid good money. We convinced them that they owed us, so they came to the house one night. And it was such a surprise, Wayne Jackson and Andrew Love, tenor sax and trumpet, a white guy and a black guy. Such a rare thing in Memphis. And they filled the song with this whole loud attitude, nasty and soulful.

I went to turn down the sax some—the sax was a kind of bully, a showoff of the worst kind in the wrong mouth, masturbatory—and I accidentally pushed delete. It asked me if I was sure. The question was blinking and I felt a sudden urgency. I got up and shut his door. I lay down on my stomach, stared down and pushed yes.

I took out the saw too, which always distracted me, then the viola, the ugly cousin of the stringed instruments. The elementary class had to go—far too much treble. The sound of tires on gravel was nice in itself, but wasn't it just an overproduction, predictably odd? Washboards—gone. Sure, it was great to get back to the roots—bluegrass *is* one of America's purest forms. But to abandon subtlety? To feature it for a whole measure, like a badge that says, "See, mountain music is not obsolete." What do any of us do to deserve these things at all? I went through, stripping song after song. But there was still too much. I erased everything.

I felt like I had finished a fistfight. It wasn't all guilt. It was like the first action I had done in a long time. I couldn't quit pacing his room. I started cleaning. I separated his laundry. Then I went to the washer and did a load for him. It was thrilling to think of what he'd say, to imagine the intensity of the future argument.

Then I thought of him leaving the house for good, without saying goodbye. I took a cup of coffee from that morning and poured it on the machine, but it kept working. I brewed some more and dumped the whole pot on the board until it fried.

———

A month later, when I was finally able to show myself in his house, Guy said he had never believed the coffee was an accident. The guy at the repair shop told him. But Guy was not as mad as I thought he'd be. In fact, he was so calm that I asked him how he did it.

"One, I had it all saved on my computer. Two, you'll buy me a new machine. But, I think you might be right. Not about deleting it all—that was a real dick move. The songs could be simpler. Think of it: Hendrix and the Experience, Cream, Nirvana, or even the quartet. You can do it all in three or four pieces. Plus, I've got to admit. It was fun to see you squirm to cover it up. How is the new place?"

"Different. I can hear the overpass. The one I showed you on YouTube. I spray painted it. BRIDGE TOO SHORT. I don't think it helped. Sometimes, I'm in the house and I hear this crash."

"Are you having a breakdown?" he asked.

"I'm getting things organized. I became flabby. In my brain. I am tutoring two kids in math. I thought there would be like twenty who'd sign up. Just two kids from Florida Street. All bright-eyed."

"Going to be the great white father then?"

"No. But they help me understand math again."

"Did you really think you could get rid of my music that easy?"

"I'm not a good dude, Guy. Not like I always thought. I had to blow everything up." It had all come so naturally, like all the pathways in my body had said I should do it, sent the bolt of protein onto the synaptic cleft and opened up the axons, and it just flowed.

81

Guy wanted to have some dinner together and was frying steak and veggies in a wok. He was pretty proud of the wok and cleaned it and rubbed it with light oil even before he sat down for us to eat. I wandered into the house looking at the things there, thinking one day I'd miss this whole time in my life. This whole stupid self I'd become. I called to Guy in the kitchen that I was going to a movie. He was surprised but just waved.

I went to the newly redone outdoor mall on the Square hoping to see the new Japanese action film where the fighters seem to fly, bouncing on the tops of bamboo trees. I needed a little magic. If you think about fixed patterns too much you wonder how we get anywhere new anyway. And so, it is important to stick your tongue out at these facts, and so maybe Diane was right that Einstein was the right poster.

I was early so I walked to the side of the theater. They'd redone the Shell Auditorium next door. It'd been where Elvis first played. And Johnny Cash, who must have been up there all confident with his big mouth and voice, and ability to read a crowd. The backdrop was all glowing and round like the mouth of clam, the performer as the pearl in the middle. We sometimes think the spotlight should be for us. At least I had.

I walked back to go in the movie and saw Diane in line with a guy. He was short and had a goatee. They were standing just to the side of the line; he pointed at the marquee in the middle. I thought of turning back; she hadn't seen me.

"Diane," I said and waved as I approached the line.

She paused, looked at her friend. I walked up and

stood next to her.

"Going to a movie, Charlie?" she said.

"The Japanese one."

Her friend put out his hand and I shook it and introduced myself. Her friend said, "Jeferey with one 'F'. That's the one we got, too. I think it is Chinese though."

I nodded. "Oh. Right. Of course."

I held my ticket like it was a permission slip and told them 'bye. They came right behind me. In the candy line, I offered to buy them chocolate. "She likes the Goobers, Jeff. Then mixing it in with the popcorn." I did not give him time to respond and said, "Crazy, right? But, you'll be surprised. The soft and the crunch. The salt and sweet."

Diane started to pull him back from me in line. "Thanks, Charlie. We are good. Enjoy the show."

She walked away with him, but I didn't think I could follow them into the movie. I wondered how she'd moved on like that. And suddenly I felt very proud of her. And I wondered at just how well we all do. Find people who need the same things we do. Someone who, if they do dislike one of your favorite things, does so in an interesting way. Someone who accepts the realities of a moment. Even with everyone's shit. We have a bit of tilt, asymmetry built right in there. And yet here we are, moving in, being adopted, making babies, stringing together new bits of future.

## Germantown Players Club

Try having sex in a shower with your pregnant wife with no close walls to grab onto! Try drying your hands on towels with initials so fancy that you can't read them. Try balancing your plate on your knees after deciding that, really, that red teak dinner table should not be used by common house sitters.

I had pretty well memorized my principal's house, but I still questioned which driveway was which. All houses with the new trends of blocky stone façades in random shards, Brady-Bunch style, the windows of the next house right there, as if in a stoic conversation. Magda said she could imagine the neighbors lining up at the nicer Home Depot one weekend for the same things. I calculated the twenty years it would take before the houses would need a whole new neighborhood, that much farther away from inner Memphis, from the trash, away from city taxes for city schools that still won't have enough.

Magda and I were good house sitters. Our principal's husband kept fish, some prized triggerfish that were still swimming around, kissing the glass with their big faces. He'd sprung for the more expensive seawater tank for the foyer. Beautiful. Even the sand-colored flounder, with its two eyes on the same side staring up from the bottom, had a kind of poetry. I taught biology at the middle

84

school and was always seeing things in the way nature is put together. This neighborhood was a flounder, I'd told Magda, that chooses to only see one side of the fence. She tolerated my little stabs at wisdom. She'd been there at the crappy hospital when everything went wrong. We'd always be on the same team that way, walking around with what happened, teaching young kids, while we missed what we should have.

The country club reality was having one full bathroom for every resident in the house, and it makes one blind. They would not be able to see or smell the facts of our school, where when, during the previous week, the toilets broke, and I had to lead the kids two by two into the janitor's closet to the mop drain and bucket. At first, the kids thought it was fun, until the line kept stretching out and the girls were getting nervous, and we took most of a class to go to the bathroom.

The triggers were making nice spins and bubbles toward the food that floated down. When I went on and on about the flounder, Magda said she was getting tired of my speeches and told me to go outside and cool off. I stood in the driveway looking at the garages. Our boss Dr. Eleanor Freese and her man had three garage doors but only two cars. Maybe I wanted spare cars too, extra doors, more cabinets than I had pans for. Our principal was married to a big timer at FedEx, and so the administration job for her was more like a hobby. At least she was good at it. I hoped her husband knew it, that what she did wasn't just spare time. Did he know how quaint shipping iPads felt to someone who was making sure poor Memphis kids could read?

I walked to the street, which was empty and quiet.

There were speed bumps to slow down teenagers. It was fall, and you could feel it on your arms. I thought of my birthday that was coming up, and how surprising it is that we are all born and how Magda talks about how amazing it is that the female body makes eyes and skin. The county fair would be starting up, and that's where I'd always had my birthday parties. Corn dogs, funnel cakes, throw-up rides that aren't safe. We'd pile onto Elvis's favorite roller coaster, the Zippin Pippin, a wooden job more thrilling because of its propensity to break down than for speed. My mom would eye the rides nervously while handing out the piles of tickets to my friends and cousins.

I went to check the mail, and there were two brick mailboxes next to each other on the opposite side of the street, as if mail itself was unsightly. I checked the one I thought was the Freeses' but there wasn't anything there. I checked the other to make sure I had the right one. On top, there was a magazine—*AJOG*, American Journal of Obstetrics and Gynecology. There was a picture of some purple cells dividing, floating down a pink canal on a black background. The lead article was called "Infant Neurological Development: Omega-3s Revisited." I opened it up and started reading, leaning on the cool brick mailbox. It talked about mitosis and how things keep halving to make more, and I started to think about how I could show it to the eighth graders in my class, a little construction paper, some glue.

A huge Chevy Suburban honked its horn at me. It startled me. When I flinched, I dropped the magazine and the rest of the mail. I picked it up, feeling a guilty rush of blood to my head. In the truck, a man in green scrubs stared at me, his wrist relaxed over the top of the steering wheel, like a hip-hop star.

He rolled down the window. "What's going on?"

"House sitting," I said, as if I could not complete a full sentence. I pointed at the house.

"At my mailbox?"

"There was an article on Omega-3s," I said, showing him the cover. I handed it out to him, along with the rest.

He stared at the mail like it was laced with arsenic. He took it. "You know these folks?"

"Dr. Eleanor Freese is my principal, a graduate of the University of Tennessee-Knoxville."

"Doctor. Right." He held up the magazine. "These things. A lot of doctor gibberish in here, ain't it?"

I could tell he was putting on his best twang, hey, I relate to you, doctor's voice.

"Sounds like Omega-3s aren't as good as they thought." Magda and I had been paying attention to the pregnancy books. We thought we were doing right this time.

"Well, they stimulate axon-to-axon communication. Like grease on gears. Keep that train a-movin'. Sounds pretty good to me."

"That's not what they say. The fish oil contains mercury inhibitors, which can poison as many axons as they stimulate."

"Of course, you don't mess with that fish oil stuff. Get the prescription. The veggie Omegas. No problemo."

"Yeah, no problem. Why don't all those poor mothers just go to Walgreens, skip the rent and just fill the fucking prescription? No big whoop."

"Nice attitude. Just stay out of my mailbox, okay."

"Yours. It's all you and yours and your stupid truck."

I stepped on the rail to his truck and tried to reach in and grab the magazine back from the dash. He knocked my face with the hard edge of his palm. And I stumbled off the step, my eyes watering. I felt weak to have been pushed so easily. Some nonperson. A kid being tossed around by an uncle.

"We have a right to this information." I touched my face, being overdramatic about the nature of the injury. Maybe he would worry about a lawsuit.

"You come anywhere near me or my house again, and you'll be dealing with the police. I got no time for your socialism this evening."

He started driving up into his driveway and I kicked his fender. He shook his head and kept going. I watched his garage door open and close in an impressively smooth motion.

I walked back to our front door, which was glass in different triangles like crystal. I could see my face in the center of one diamond. There wasn't much of a mark. I decided I'd avoid telling Magda if I could. It was so quiet in the house I wondered if she was still there or if she'd seen me through the window. I wondered if she ever had the urge to run away, find some calmer man. She could get into one of these Mercedes and drive away.

Magda was in the kitchen leaning close to the oven to see how high the flame was. She adjusted it.

"These mother fuckers actually think they deserve all this," I said.

"I thought you were going to cool it," she said. We'd

enjoyed using the gas burners that whole weekend even as we tried not to make a mess. I could smell that she was cooking something with a lot of cumin.

"I was just checking the mail. I saw the neighbor's stuff. A doctor guy. His mail had a journal talking about babies. He's some gynecologist. I wanted to read it. He didn't have to get so fucking offended."

"Did you tell him I was pregnant?"

"Shit. That would've got him." I moved to go outside. She grabbed my arm and pointed me back to the stove.

"Leave it. Just avoid him. He probably thought you were stealing."

"I fooled the guards at the gate to do a little mail fraud."

"What would you do? Have a beer with the guy holding your stuff? You can't go around arguing with people when the kid gets here. Ugh. You're going to make me have this baby on a golf course." She laughed and loaded a wooden spoon. "I wonder if they make the ambulance drivers sign in at the gate. Taste this." She held out some charro beans that she'd started on last night. It was the way her mom made it and they had a lot of great natural folate, which were said to absorb better than the folic acids they pump in prenatal pills.

"Yum." They really were something. When Magda and I first got together, my family had said stupid things, like "You eat beans for breakfast?" Now, I couldn't imagine breakfast without them. "I'll be better," I said.

"What did the magazine say?" she asked, grabbing her stomach. She said she liked being pregnant. She felt around, seeing if the baby was moving.

"It will go okay, this time," I said.

"What did it say?"

"Fish oil. Those new pills I got are junk."

"Shit. This is a big brain month, too."

"He said we should get some vegetable ones."

"Assholes. Why doesn't anybody ever tell you anything?" I hugged her close. I could tell she was not mad at him, just all of it. I could see outside the window into the guy's back yard. The doctor was throwing a tennis ball to a golden retriever whose fur was more red than gold. The guy had a plastic ball thrower that the retriever would drop the slobbery ball into. I'd always hated the feel of spit and slime, and having to tug at the dog's hot mouth. He had a glass of white wine on the next table and was talking to a woman who shook her head at something he said.

Nine days, our last baby had lived. We'd gone to the wrong hospital, I think, and they hadn't paid attention. It was a whole week of wondering if Magda would be all right or if the baby would or if they both wouldn't. And now at least Magda was here and we were close again.

We'd named the baby Aída after Magda's mother, even though my parents pronounced it wrong. This time, we weren't sharing the name. It was living quietly in our heads. This time, we were paying out of pocket for the better hospital. I wondered about the guy next door, what network he was in. His hands seemed so relaxed. Even the bit of karate had been measured and precise. Just enough. A little harder and he might have hurt his hand, or broken my nose. I liked that he was still reading. Some of the teachers at my school would graduate from college and never read or assign anything new. The guy was on top of his stuff. Maybe I could re-introduce myself.

I was resting my face in Magda's hair, which was getting warm in my breath. I tried not to move even though I'd started to cry some. Her hair had gotten this beautiful sheen again, like last time. We were pressed against each other and I could feel the baby jerking, hiccupping maybe. Maybe she would be a shortstop like her mother, a beautiful thing running in the beautiful light. Past the guy's house, all you could see was green. It stretched out in different shades, past the putting green, down the fairway, up into the tall oaks that lined the left side of the fairway. It went across the knobby hills that fed down a small creek down to the right side that fed a pond. A sweet gum had turned red, and red leaves spread out in the water, floating. Lots of space and clumps and rings shooting out from the evening fish. Just a beautiful time of day.

# Little Pigeon River

Jacob was the one who suggested the open marriage. It would cause a crisis, a crisis that would produce change and a subsequent opportunity to open up new aspects of the human personality. He intellectualized it this way. To Tonja, he'd brought up the bonobo monkeys. Everyone sleeps with everyone and so they have less murder. Less possessive dudes prowling the bushes smashing the skulls of other people's kids. That's how your average chimp would behave. But the bonobos were led by savvy females with sexual power. Having slept with each other and with a few of the men, they would have the dudes feeling confused, quite calm, and have them lying dopey in the sun. The clan would govern in a kind of sexual trance, decently following each other around, all coked up on oxytocin and sex and eating a lot of fruit.

"You just want some ass," Tonja'd said. She was from Los Angeles, and every so often would say something to the point with an urban kind of verve, and it still surprised Jacob, so used to living in places like Knoxville and the South with its politeness and conditional phrasing.

Most of the time her directness was accurate. When he'd been reading about the bonobos in the *National Geographic* in his office at the university, he'd gotten an erection. Thinking about several sexual encounters in one day, fielding the advances of confident women. Of eating fruit, watching two or three women satisfy each other on some rock or another, their using the raised surface as a kind of sexual tool for sound positioning. Even the thought of seeing a trusted male buddy fuck (his head had switched to this language now) a former companion seemed a splendid way to spend an afternoon. Of being invited over to them with the buddy's long gaze and slipping in. Anything could happen in confusion. Any blessed thing.

Only, when Tonja actually found someone, his theories disappeared from under him, and he had to admit he was a chimp or a chump or just some early hominid.

Tonja told him about the guy when she got tipsy at a party they went to for her law firm, and in front of everyone she talked about her new lover. Her firm had just won a major election against a union and rented a private suite at the Smokies baseball game to celebrate. Around the sixth inning, Jacob was enjoying the keg beer and the cool night air and sitting next to Gary Glimmer, a hefty partner who commented on everything but the game.

"I've been thinking of shaving off my mustache." Gary put his finger over his mustache, trying to hide it. "What do you think?"

"I don't know, Gary. I think you're stuck with that thing." The field was well lit and each player had three shadows of various depths. Tonja finally sat down by him to watch the last few innings and said she'd forgotten how much she liked Canadian whisky. He ignored her; since her new "arrangement," he was practicing disaffection. She told him to look at her. He asked Gary what kind of grass he thought they used for the field.

93

"Jacob, you big shot." Tonja spoke loud, and the people around them straightened up, listening but pretending not to.

"Watch the game."

She smiled. "You've met Ray Krueger."

Krueger was the managing partner. Jacob saw him inside the private suite, standing on a chair adjusting a floodlight. He was a big guy, handsome face, kind of Clooney aging in his favor. He got the light centered on a painting and got off the chair. Another lawyer gave him a high-five.

"He loves to go down on me, Jacob." Tonja killed the rest of her drink.

People stared outright, some offended. There was a kid not far off. They'd never wanted kids themselves, and both sometimes forgot they were around

Jacob stood up to leave. "Think of the kids with that mouth of yours. No telling where it's been." She did look over and mouthed sorry to the woman. Jacob shook his head like a Puritan and left for the car, hoping she would come after him.

————

After the baseball game, Jacob began an aggressive search for an interested young student. Suddenly it felt like he'd started a race he was losing badly.

Finding an interested student was much harder than he thought. To his attractive students, he wrote open-ended questions on their assignments. To Amber Prine, he wrote, "This is a highly suggestive rationale; let's discuss." To Courtney Regan, "*Time* magazine did an amazing layout of this dig; come by the office for a copy?" He started wearing his wedding ring on a cord around his neck and scratched out all the mentions of his wife from his lecture notes.

During class, a girl named April raised her hand. She had a soft voice and dreadlocks down to the small of her back. He hadn't heard her whole argument because of her soft voice, so he said, "I hope everyone made a note of that." He remembered the faculty database had said April was a junior (twenty-two?) and the president of Amnesty International. "I'm afraid we're short on time, April," he said. "Maybe we can discuss it after." *After*, he thought as the class gathered folders. Discuss shale oil in the bask, like a hot cigarette.

As the class left, Jacob saw her walking deliberately down the stairs waiting for the class to clear. He erased the board and wanted to seem surprised that she was still there.

"Oh, April," he said. She always wore long-sleeved T-shirts, and he hoped there weren't tracks under there. He did not know what dreadlocks meant these days. "About shale. Sure there's a chemical process to getting the oil from kerogen. But the real deal is all the water it takes. And then this toxic water on the back end, man. It's brutal. Here." He opened the book to them and was relieved to see her wave her hand, don't bother.

"I've actually got to go to work." She started for the door.

"Where do you work?" he asked.

She said she worked at the Falafel Hut, and Jacob

told her how he loved falafel when he stayed in Saudi Arabia, but she didn't ask about that like he hoped, only left.

————

That night, he went to the Falafel Hut and April was behind the counter. An older man with dark hair with one circle of white hair on his crown counted dollar bills next to her. Jacob went there expecting the restaurant to have an oriental design, but the place was done up as a diner with autographed photos of local sports heroes and a big Davy Crockett guy painted on the wall. He sat down at the front counter and he and April chatted while he ate. His sandwich was good; the sauce tasted like homemade tahini. He complained about the spanakopita.

"Yeah," she said. "John gets those from Sam's." The restaurant was empty, so she started shucking garlic and talking about how he took great pains with the falafel but not much else. With the edge of a knife, she would break the shell and use her fingernail to twist the rest off.

"He's an alcoholic," she said, "and he's always wanting me to take shots with him while we're closing. Creepy old men." She leaned forward, sharing the joke.

Jacob felt awkward. "Can I try some?" he asked. She put half of the garlic in a bowl, gave him a plate and wooden wicker basket for the waste.

He watched her more closely and imitated.

She stopped and breathed in as if shocked and said, "Have you heard what they want to do to the Turkey Creek wetlands?"

Jacob hadn't heard but said, "Shocking business." In his experience, there could be only one reason to talk about a wetland.

"You should come to the protest. The news trucks might come out, and it would be good for them to interview someone like you, an expert and all."

"I'm definitely into that," he said. He told her a story about wetlands. How you could put totally contaminated water on one end, DDT and all, and by the time it got to the other end, it becomes fresh again. They became quiet, just the rip of garlic skin, and he thought of Tonja when they were young. He and she had been through this ground already, and he felt glad that his old knowledge now seemed new again. With Tonja, though, he told her all his minor anecdotes, and Tonja had him pegged as an average professor and fairly unimpressive. He wanted to be like April seemed—her clear understanding of what she wanted.

"Let's all have a drink," John said and went to the front door and locked it. Coming back, he reached under the counter and brought out tequila and glasses. They cheered each other but she didn't take hers. She held it out, leaning with her other arm on the island.

"Come out with me, April." Jacob put his glass down. "Show me where you all like to go."

"Great. Another creep," she said.

"I like to think of myself as one of those bonobos. You ever hear about them. They make peace through love," he said.

"Love. That's the fancy word for it." She took the

shot, put it on the counter. "Now, if anyone asks, tell them I am just a woman trying to get a degree," she said to both of the men staring at her. "A gal can't just be nice these days. It has to mean something."

Jacob stayed for a while, then said 'bye.

When he got home, he went into Tonja's working studio where she had the designs for an upcoming union election. She hated overhead lights, so a cracked desk lamp was on the floor beside her. It lit up her face and threw a long shadow of her across the room. She used to get frustrated because the male lawyers expected her to do the artsy-type work, but now she liked it more than writing the briefs.

"What do you think?" she asked, not turning around. She was chewing some ice, which was loud in the big room. She got in zones while she was in her work, and he hated breaking them. On the top of a finished T-shirt "Vote No!" was written, and in the center a man in a hard hat stood cock-kneed with his hands on his head in shock. The pockets of his jeans were hanging out and empty.

"A message for me." He laughed.

She stood and went over to look out the window. "Why is it when you give up on your job, you mull out in this fucking depression and all of a sudden it's my fault? All of a sudden it's the relationship that is the problem."

He followed her and stood behind her. It was true; he'd stopped doing real research when he got tenure. He did not even care if he ever became a full professor. Writing a bunch of articles about water salinity, very well done, very precise, that ultimately produced nothing new to the world.

Her old car was in the driveway, the light from the carport shining on it. The dent in the door looked bigger with the shadow. He rested his head on the hardest part of her skull. "When you said relationship just now, it sounded like a relation is a ship."

She did not smile.

"You used to laugh at those kind of dumb things I said."

"Yeah."

"Should we get divorced like other people?" he said.

She turned quickly and he let his head hit the window. He went over towards her, looking at the floor as if in trouble.

Looking up at him, she drew her finger, still wet with paint, across his cheek, and went back to her stool. "As strange as it sounds, Jacob, this is working for me." She took up a mixing bowl and stirred it. "You and Ray are both pretty cool in your own ways."

He wanted to scream. Instead, he sanded a bureau she wanted to repaint, and eventually got into the rhythm of it, scouring it loudly, so that she made some comment, but he kept on watching the paint dull, hoping it had a bit of lead in it somewhere.

————————

The protesters met up in the K-mart parking lot down the road from Turkey Creek. Young kids had signs made and handed out flyers, and when the cameras came people bunched together to orchestrate a sense of crowd.

April, it seemed to Jacob, tried to hit up every customer with the flyer and a spiel and wasn't paying him much attention. He'd hoped she would be by his side listening to the well-thought-out reasons he'd come up with. She would hear and look up to that part of him, but she was always doing some other damned thing.

He could've kissed her, though, during his interview with a pretty black reporter who had a bandana around her neck. In the middle of his rant, April straightened his T-shirt for the camera to read. It was one he got with Tonja at La Veta Pass at a water study—kokopelli, a trickster fertility god to the Hopi playing flute on a mountain. "Yeah, kokopelli," Jacob said and smiled. He put an arm around April and pulled her into the camera shot and said, "Walk with Beauty."

After a while April went off with her friends, but Jacob didn't want to share her anymore that day. Her friends told him about a rafting trip the next weekend, and April invited him, squeezing his arm. He felt like the cool teacher. On the way home, Jacob thought, that's the clip they'll use—both of them smiling.

———

Jacob picked April up for white-water tubing the next weekend. She sat on the porch and hopped up when she heard him honk. She had shaved her head and the new skin showed an uneven tan up top. They were going to follow her friends in his car, and Jacob was glad for the chance to get to know her better. She talked for a while about religion and family, both of which she resented. She went on for a while about motherhood and conventions, then stopped herself.

"Every time I open my mouth, I show how young I am," she said.

He rubbed her shaved head, feeling it spike against the grain. "Why'd you shave it?" He'd liked the dreadlocks. The shaved head made her look hungry. He put his hand back on the gear even though they were on the highway. They were going past a soybean field and he could smell the chemicals.

"I had a fucked-up night," she said.

"I've been thinking of cutting mine."

"I like curly hair." She tried to run her fingers through it, but they got stuck, and they laughed.

She dug in her bag for a CD. Out of the back of a Cubs T-shirt, her bathing suit strap was tied around her neck. For the first time he saw her forearms. Pink scar tissue rose in rows of four and crisscrossed each other. When she reached to put in a CD, he felt her arms.

She looked down and took away her arm. "Old."

He cracked the window. "They're not that old. If you ever want to talk ... ." They had made it to National Park now, and a van full of relatives took pictures by the road sign. He showed her his right hand that had an old scar across the pinky. "When I was in college, I had an ex-girlfriend who didn't call me on my birthday. About four in the morning, I went over to her house, but it was dark so I figured she was asleep. The screen door was locked, so I had to cut a hole in it. I was knocking on her door so hard the window shattered. I could've walked in at that point, but I felt so stupid."

"I don't break other people's things."

"I probably seem like I'm all together to you. I think most people are like that though—barely holding on."

She told a story of her fiancé. He was an Olympic medalist in the butterfly; only she told this fact without joy, because once he became famous and made money selling cereal, he had called it off. Jacob remembered the guy from TV; everyone started calling him Dash, which had amused Jacob even though it was a marketing thing.

The river was low, and the sun reflected off it harshly. Low water meant difficult tubing. Jacob said, "Remember how I said in class that one day people will go to war over things like fresh water instead of oil. That doesn't really worry me. In my heart, I worry that we will have so many big problems like thirst, that we will not even get to pay attention to our finer problems."

"Like self-pity." April took off her sunglasses and put them on his face. "And love." The glasses were vintage and white, clownish, and the frames put pressure on his head. They were quiet for a while.

When they got to the drop-in, her friends halved bourbon and Dr. Pepper in plastic liter bottles and stepped into the icy river. Jacob didn't drink himself, but propped himself up on the tube and had a large time floating and dodging rocks. The cold water did wonders to April's nipples, as if there was no bikini at all. He laughed with the others when they dropped their drinks or lost contact lenses. Halfway down, the light streamed in orange lines through the trees.

They stopped for a break and sat on dry rocks, and

he felt warm from the full sun, like a lizard. The kids started passing around some dope and cheese that a tall guy with glasses had been carrying in a belt pouch. One couple, the two most attractive, went off from the group and were kissing behind a small bush; clearly they wanted everyone to see that they were skilled. Jacob toked a bit, and the tall guy asked Jacob about trout. Jacob said their scientific name and April urged him on with a pretend clap. He told them about how the human hand touching a trout is like battery acid. That you have to wet your hand to touch them.

"It's a good metaphor, yes. For our relationship to nature. We are the disease but don't have to be." Everyone stopped laughing, and Jacob realized they probably wanted to hear something happier.

They got back in, and eventually, the river became all shadow; Jacob could see the riverbed more clearly without the reflection. The rocks were freckled and smooth at the bottom, settled like eggs even in the push of the water. Pigeon is the right name for this river, he thought.

They got out of the water where they'd left the guy's van. Jacob and April shared a towel and made fun of their goose bumps and pale skin. They squeezed each other's knees and arms, both swearing they couldn't feel a thing.

Jacob liked being the designated driver and insisted that April ride shotgun. How responsible she must think me, he thought. We seem like a couple already, sharing the tired sighs of a vacation, a walk through the woods that's always twenty minutes too long.

"The roads didn't seem that curvy on the way in." April talked in her low, soft voice, so only he could hear it—that it was for him alone, her realization that even a slight change in an angle of the light made the world seem different.

They dropped him off at his car. They were camping for a few days and going rock climbing. She stood with him at his car while he put on a T-shirt and dry shoes. She made fun of his T-bird, saying environmentalists should have hybrids. He said he liked driving a manual, and he pointed to his bike rack on the back.

"I ride to work most of the time. In fact," he reached in the back and got out his helmet, "wear this when you climb, please."

She held it, turning it over in her hands. It was gold streaked with silver. He realized he'd given her Tonja's helmet, the lightning bolts a little swirly and feminine. "I'll try." She kissed him 'bye, but it was so brief—one she might give a brother or dear uncle. He told her to take care.

————

When Jacob got back to Tonja's—it had become her house in his mind—he asked her to get drunk with him.

"You prefer it quiet, Jacob," she said. She sat on the kitchen island and motioned for him to lean back between her knees. The light over the stove shined on the slick tiled counters. The tile had been a summer project, and they sweated together and argued about the proper consistency of the mortar. Those had been useful conflicts—basic problem solving—and it had been easy for them not to hurt each other's feelings. Those people were gone now.

She hooked her legs around him and beat time on his chest.

"I do like the quiet," he said, feeling old and worn out.

"We'll pull out the foldout bed in the couch." She bent and kissed his ear and it was loud.

He sighed and leaned back against her.

"I downloaded four movies you haven't seen." She hit his chest harder and they got up and set up the den. She said it would be like their camping days. He kept falling asleep lying next to her on the stiff springy foldout. When he roused, she would press pause and explain the plot of the movie, the mood and composition of the pictures, and he would sleep again then wake, and she'd explain.

―――――――

Jacob wasn't surprised that April missed class on Monday, but when she didn't show up for the rest of the week, he got worried and walked over to her house after Friday's class. It was a white house with an L-shaped porch. The balcony was missing some rails and slanted from right to left. A black Lab barked at him, and Jacob backed up then saw a Frisbee with teeth marks on the sides. He threw the Frisbee to the side yard but the dog didn't move. He went onto the porch; the dog still barked, but it looked scared too.

April's roommate Cheryl opened the door and yelled at the dog. "You're her teacher. From the river."

"Is April home?" he asked over the dog's barking.

"Shit, you don't even know." She motioned for him to enter. She had her hand on the dog's collar, and it was licking her wrist. She let him go when Jacob was in the door, and as they climbed the stairs, she told him how they had been climbing all the first morning when April lost her foothold. She'd been new to it and held her own for a while, but her strength gave out and she fell from two stories.

"She's going to make it," Cheryl said. "She tore all the ligaments in her left knee. Her left wrist and elbow have hairline fractures. They'll take the longest to heal." Cheryl shook her head and knocked lightly on a bedroom door. Jacob followed her in.

April's limbs all had casts and braces, and her face was all bruised and cut. "Ouch," he said.

"I know," Cheryl said and patted him on the shoulder and shut the door as she left.

He went to her bedside. He felt along the soft cast on her leg. Her arms were propped up on pillows, and the desk by the bed had gauze, novels, and medication. Her face was scratched up, which made her look vulnerable in the full light from the window by the bed, like Joan of Arc. She was sleeping. The blinds were up and he imagined her looking outside most of the day, feeling lonely and scared. He would buy her a bird book, an illustrated Sibley edition, almost like art. He would care for her and pity her and read her the names and behavior of the migrating warblers and tanagers.

He pulled her office chair around and stared at her. On the desk she had a black rotary phone like in movies. He picked it up and dialed, listening to it click. He called Tonja—they were supposed to take their cat Alfred to the vet. During the past week, the cat had been eating its own fur. Jacob talked quietly, and April took deep breaths, eyes twitching behind her lids; she was out cold. Tonja was drafting a brief for the NLRB. They talked about Alfred and the weekend, and she asked him what he was doing.

"I'm with April right now, Tonja. She fell off a mountain. She looks so sweet."

"Maybe it's time, Jacob. We're both interested in other people."

April mumbled something. Her bulletin board had articles tacked on it about Dash, and Jacob had this sudden anger at that asshole sitting around his house with all those medals. "Let's not end it like that. Tell me a story: a good one. From when you liked me."

"I can't remember that far back," she said.

He didn't say anything, just waited.

"Okay. We're on the beach at sunrise. Out on the Yucatan there are jellyfish and dolphins and you told a story about the Gulf."

"Tell it right." He traced the lines on April's shoulder brace.

"We walked towards the pink haze." She enunciated like Orson Wells. "A hundred jellyfish had washed ashore in the evening tempest. We figure-eighted between the bodies; I acted like I would push you in them. You buried one for an unsuspecting jogger."

Jacob picked a bit of fuzz out of April's short hair.

Tonja said, "The sun was pink diamonds on the water. You pointed to the Gulf and told me the story of how the world had ended out there one time. Dinosaurs die, mammals take over. I told you how sailors used to cut up starfish until they found out that all the pieces make more starfish. You said you were happy."

"One of those *Journey to Ixtlan* nature moments," he said.

In her normal voice, she said, "You were happy because you were with me."

"Can you think of me as I was then and not now?" he asked.

"You wanted this, Jacob. For fuck's sake, you always forget that." She hung up the phone.

April was still asleep. He got a marker from the desk and started drawing a starfish on her knee. He scratched it out, and it looked better that way. He got close to her face, and could feel her musty breath on his cheek. She mumbled but he didn't move. When she opened her eyes, he kissed her. She yawned, and there was a rush of hot air.

"Thank you for the helmet," she said. "Do I look awful?"

He kissed her again, deeply.

She asked for some water, and he fixed her some. She sipped through the straw but some water spilled down her neck. He set the water aside and moved closer, kissing where the water had left a trail, and kept kissing her clothes, then he kissed her chest and moved down her body and then stopped at her legs.

"Gentle," she said.

He moved her legs apart, and she winced, her face tightening up, eyes closed. She told him to hold on a second then relaxed her face and nodded, her cheeks red. He kissed her thighs and tried to move only his face. He used techniques that Tonja liked. She didn't move at all but got into it, becoming moist and making noise.

"Your roommate will hear you," he whispered.

"Shut up, Jacob." When she was finished, he hovered over her as if doing a push-up. "Wipe your mouth," she said.

He got to his knees between her legs, took off his shirt and wiped his mouth. He was over her again and slowly let his body weight down onto her.

"That's enough," she said.

"It won't take long."

"What about your wife?" she asked.

"How did you ..."

"I'm not stupid, Jacob, just younger."

"It's all over with Tonja. I want you," he said and tried to kiss her, but she jerked her head away.

"Get off me," she said, avoiding his kisses. "I'm not having sex with you."

She looked beautiful angry. "I don't understand. We just ..."

"I'm in a bad place right now," she said, starting to cry but looking away as if not. "Dash called when he heard. We're kind of talking again."

"April, *I'm* going to be here for you. We'll make a real go of it." He kissed her dramatically, as they did in movies, feeling that they had really started something.

She bit him hard on the lip and held it.

He jumped up, and she screamed in pain.

"What the fuck?" he said and checked his lip, which was bleeding.

"Get out." She yelled now and tried to stand up, which made her cry more in pain. "I'm just supposed to go gooey around you. And you don't even know me. Want to be my daddy. You're a liar and ... and a student fucker." She cried hard and it frustrated her when she couldn't move. "Get out. Please, Jacob. I don't know. Just get out."

When he went into the hall, he almost ran into Cheryl who had a tennis racket in her hand. They stared at each other while he went down the stairs. I won't run out, he thought. Then he heard the dog out front. He opened the door, took the three porch steps in one bound and jumped the gate. He'd not jumped anything in probably ten years.

Outside, the air was cool. He kept running and taking side streets and didn't know which one he was on. Walking up a hill, he took long strides, and the roots of an oak tree broke up the concrete. He was out of breath and leaned against the tree. He felt along his lip, which was swelling and numb. On the intersection ahead, a convenience store looked open. A man wheeled a shopping cart full of cans up the street and waited in front of the store for customers' change.

Jacob straightened and walked towards the store and waved to the homeless man.

"You need cans?" Jacob asked. "I've got cans at home. Bags of them. Follow me to the house and we'll get the cans."

The man made a 180-degree turn with the cart, the cans settling with a noise. Jacob thought he was walking slow and noticed he had a bad left front wheel. Jacob said, "This is really important work. Forty cans save a gallon of gas." The man nodded.

Jacob said, "It's important to try, right? I mean

making these  cans takes up 3 percent of our energy resources, you know?"

"Five bucks for a hundred cans."

"Damn right. It ought to be more. Someone ought to give you a lot."

Jacob recognized the street they were on now; it was called Magnolia but was lined with big oak trees. They'd be at his house soon. From both sides of the road, the streetlights came on, and they both looked up. As they walked away from the lights, they each had two shadows out before them. The man said it was the coolest night yet. Going up an incline, a garbage bag fell out, and the man grabbed it and threw it over his shoulder. The orange light shined through the plastic lining the edges. The man looked unearthly, Jacob thought, carrying a bag of gold like some saint or a person come back from the future.

# Wall Doxey

Leonard got to the tenth hole at the Frisbee golf course at Wall Doxey State Park and looked over across the lake at the swing sets but couldn't hear them. Technically, he was not allowed to actually go into areas with kids anymore and he didn't, technically. It wasn't just the court order or his modular counselor's rules for his probation, but also a self-knowledge from months of private counseling, and so looking at the playground and not going closer gauged his growing strength. He was at his best at this Mississippi state park, alone in these tall woods, looking through their tunnel, seeing how his disk flew and seemed to hollow out a tube of air between the branches and the sky.

Number ten always forced him into that brief stare, and he wouldn't even be thinking about the kids playing there but then suddenly he would; he'd hear their high laughter skating across the lake, the busy hum of their counting down in some game, and then he'd see them there, running around on the peninsula playground, as if on a stage. Bright colors, costumed up, and pretending not to peek.

Leonard looked over and the swings were empty, rocking some in the wind. It was bitterly cold that Sunday. He turned his back, becoming interested again in his score,

112

in the next hole. Some days it was not as easy to turn away. Some days it became difficult to not just stay there and watch them, to hunker down in the weeds along the far bank and watch in privacy, maybe take out his phone and record the music. When he thought these things and still turned away, turned back into the game, back into himself and out of his mind, into his hands, the firmness of his wrist, the follow-through. These things became important to him again; he felt stronger and relieved. A better man using a second chance.

───────

Twelve was down a hill and ended at a creek bed that was always dry. It was the most secluded part of the course, where he'd sometimes see a couple of guilty-looking deer. They'd throw their heads up and look at him, and they'd jump away, picking their way gracefully through ankle-breaking brush. When he finished up his putt, the chain Frisbee net ringing in the empty woods, he paused and looked farther up the creek where he'd last seen deer running.

Just as he was ready to head toward thirteen, he saw something pink among the fallen leaves piled up along the bank. At first he figured it was a lost Frisbee, albeit a really bad throw. He picked his way down the creek wall and climbed the other side toward where he'd seen the pink. As he got closer, he saw some white, a denim color, and finally and dangerously, the color blonde. A girl about eight, unconscious, a streak of blood down her temple. Her pink coat was unzipped, falling off her shoulder. Her white T-shirt peeked through, the edge of the short-sleeved shirt, the ends ruffled, like petals. He bent to his knees, the leaves creaking and breaking under his new weight. He adjusted her coat, squeezing her shoulder like dough. With the backside of his hand he brushed the blood away from her eyelid. The blood was not yet dry and came away easily, and he kept brushing her skin, even though the blood was gone. Her skin was impossibly smooth.

He felt his face getting warmer and realized he'd gotten hard. He took off his own coat, and elevated her little legs under his coat. She was perhaps in shock. He had missed the feel of this skin. There was one area of his own leg that had never grown hair, never been exposed to any of the elements, he guessed, the hair rubbed off by his own clothes and contact. It had this kind of rich, white smoothness that none of the rest of Leonard did. He'd talked to a doctor once about it, and the man had told him to rub it when his mind was going rotten.

He eased his hand under his belt and jeans and rubbed the skin, and it helped some, paltry as it seemed next to the girl's cheek. Her hand. If her hand could touch him now. He withdrew his hand and looked back at her face, and started calling to her, poking her with a finger to wake her up. One finger, at the dead pointing end, not the palm or the tips all sultry with nerves. She was breathing through her mouth; it was open, the lips crusty and pink in the dry air. He lifted her white shirt at the edge and the new fabric revealed more petal lace, the pink of the flowers on her shirt matching the small coat, which he then removed. He put his ear on her flat chest, and the warmth felt good against his cold ear, and he left it there as if sopping it up.

Beneath the skin and shirt, he could feel her heart thump quiet, like everything else. As he raised his head, he fixed her coat and his hand lingered lightly, tracing down her chest and stomach. The light resistance felt refreshing. He'd not touched another person in so familiar a way in a very long time. He felt as if he could almost draw the newness out longer, even after he withdrew his hand, invisible connections, light coming from his fingertips, like some sorcerer movie. In the movie her flesh would keep him alive for another hundred years. He turned away from her, pressing his hands firmly against his closed eyes until there was pain and shooting light from the pressure. He looked around, his vision blurred and starred.

His uncle Gary had once talked about moments like this when Gary was quitting drinking. The moment he'd most wanted to dive back into his old booze world. He and the cargo guys from the airline he worked for were unloading a shipment, and the guy in the truck made a mistake and a crate of whiskey broke on the ground. Bourbon. Not his brand, the better one. The glass was all over, the puddle spreading out like a new storm in the sky, coming out toward his shoes, going up under them. He said the smell literally knocked him to his knees, and he had to steady himself with his hand that dipped into the oily whiskey that went onto his clothes. He brought his hand to his face and stuck his tongue out and felt its warm, numbing essence. He said that it was his proudest moment when he got up, made it to the bathroom and washed his face, not really recognizing the person staring back. Instead of lying down in the whiskey like he wanted to and letting the glass cut his skin and feeling the alcohol burn into him from all directions, he removed his wet clothes and stared hard.

Leonard could hear the highway faintly off in the distance. If one of those drivers would only launch unharmed off the highway and perform a dust-off, get-out miracle, relieving him of her. Leonard watched her breathing and thought of the mercy of her unconsciousness, how sometimes the mind goes away when it needs to. She was not even here; only he was here, which was the problem.

He could feel the strength of his erection even though he was sitting. He touched it through his jeans to feel its pressure. It wasn't like his usual ones, just enough; the girl had made him young again. He felt strong. He got up and walked over to a small tree. He turned away from the girl now and undid his pants. With himself exposed, he walked straight through and felt the branches and leaves against his penis. He kept walking, his eyes closed, winter light red against his eyelids. He ran over a sticker bush and felt them dig and draw against his skin. He held his penis now and that felt even better, still hard, his hand against the new scars. The girl came into his mind, and he opened his eyes suddenly, feeling a little dizzy from heavy breathing. The little girl in his mind still had the blood on her head, which made him stop, even though he hadn't finished. He looked down and removed a thorn and held it up, wondering if it was really him all this was happening to. He slowly turned to where the girl still lay.

He pulled up his pants and buckled his belt and felt a sudden rush, as if the emergency had only now just happened. In his hurry, he tripped on a root, and landed next to her; he did not mean to get so close again. He could feel her warmth. Her hand was out, cupped some, making the shape of the letter "c." If he took her hand and used it to help him finish, it would be over in ten seconds. She would never know.

He picked up the hand, checked the pulse, and after feeling it there, still alive, he pushed it away from him, against her own body, and he stood and screamed. The woods echoed it. He hoped someone would hear it. Had the whole world gone fucking deaf? He yelled at the trees—who lets a fucking child walk around in the goddamned woods by herself? Who in this world would ever, for even one second, let a child out of sight?

He went back over and shook the girl hard, and her little head moved loosely, as if she were an infant.

"Wake up, you fucking baby."

The noise launched out into the open woods. The leaves rolled along with a breeze. Just the white noise of the highway. He looked down at the girl. She looked peaceful enough. Her hair was a blonde mess spread out in the leaves, as if she were part of some strange altar.

He bent and arranged her hair neater. He supposed it had been wrong to move her at all. He laughed at himself, getting the last strand of hair from her eye. He picked her up, cradled her in his arms like a bride. He talked to her as he went back through the course toward the lodge where there was a ranger. Even on a slow day, there would be one in there watching *Dr. Phil.*

To the girl, he described his round that day—the good shots, the putts that against all reason went straight to the chains from fifty yards away, dropping in the basket. Her hair was falling straight to the ground. Her parents must be the kind that never cut it, or rarely, with much debate, as if it were the rarest substance in the world. Which it was. He realized he had forgotten his coat and went back to get it.

Closer to the lodge, he could see the edge of the lake, a long brown scar from where the water level was down that year, down every year it seemed. Can it ever catch up after that?

The parking lot was empty except for the ranger's pickup and Leonard's own car. Bending down, easing the child closer to the office door, he grabbed the knob and threw open the door with his foot. A large, bearded man behind the desk watched a portable TV. Neon Frisbees were displayed on the wall behind him. The man stood, looking more prepared for a Lynyrd Skynyrd concert than to hike the woods.

"Call the police. This girl needs help." Leonard went to the lounge area couch and laid the girl gently on the vinyl cushions. The ranger was on the phone quickly. The ambulance would have to come from Holly Springs, eight miles away. Leonard started regretting coming in here. Maybe he should have just left her at the door; he wondered if he had wanted to be caught. The pictures on the wall behind the girl were of the state park when it was first established. The lodge was just a small cabin then, but the lake spread out behind it, the trees healthy.

The ranger came over and checked her, feeling along her neck for a pulse. He'd brought a first aid kit, but didn't open it.

"Well, at least she's alive," he said.

Leonard told the ranger the story of finding her and calling out for help and how the girl was all alone, and except for the little bit of blood, she had seemed fine. The ranger nodded throughout, mostly looking at the girl.

"Cute kid," the ranger said, and that he hoped the ambulance would come soon. The ranger looked at Leonard for a response. The ranger stared a little longer now, seeming to look at Leonard up and down.

"Your barn door is open, guy."

Leonard looked down and turned away while he zipped it, tucking in his shirt for good measure.

"Getting pretty chilly out there, ain't it?" the ranger asked.

Leonard realized he was still holding his coat and not wearing it. He smiled without answering and went over to the water fountain. The man sat down on the edge of the couch between Leonard and the kid.

"Wonder where that ambulance could be?" Leonard asked.

This time it was the ranger who did not answer. Leonard looked down at his watch, and then realized he hadn't worn it that day.

"Gosh, I've got to get going. Wasn't planning on all this."

"Don't you want to see if she's all right?"

"Really, my wife is expecting me to pick up our kid from her mother's."

"Oh. You ought to bring your wife and child out here sometime. Frisbee is a great family thing."

Leonard moved to the door. "Yeah. My son has got

that asthma pretty bad."

"You still drive that Grand Am. The green one? I like those late-nineties models myself."

"That's the one. God. I hope she's okay." Leonard had the door open and felt the cool air against him. He was sweating profusely, he realized. It was cold. Over his shoulder, he called back, "Good luck, little girl."

───────────

He got to his car, sat down, and put the key in the ignition. He was watching the door, waiting for the overweight ranger to come after him. The lodge was still. He tucked and smoothed his shirt again. He could hear the sirens and wondered if it was just the ambulance the man had called. He wondered how he would explain the cuts on his genitals or if it would even come to that. He was pulling out of the parking lot, driving past the entrance fee booth, which was usually left empty in the winter months, putting people on the honor system. The ambulance had its lights going, although the sound was off. Leonard gave the woman driving a nod. He looked back at her in the rearview and then saw his own face. He stopped at the highway, both sides empty. To the right the highway climbed to the highest point in the county. It wasn't all that high, but you could see the highway cut into the trees before you. Green pines so close together that they made a kind of purple.

## Lottie's Dressing

Mama was in the kitchen bending over to smell the first batch of Thanksgiving dressing. "Grandmamma's dressing," she said and set it to cool next to some broken eggs that she'd put back in the carton. Mama was one of those that cleaned up the mess even while she was still making it. My dad's mom had always liked my mom best out of all the aunts and shared all her recipes. Grandmamma went a long time with only the three sons and a husband around, and when my dad brought Mama home, Grandmamma had said it felt right to have her there and took right to her, sharing all the family secrets and recipes straight out. Grandmamma wrote all dishes out in a cookbook and my mom dusted it off once a year at Thanksgiving.

I'd been bragging about Grandmamma's food to Amina when we were still at Ole Miss. We'd met up a year ago on study abroad in Wales, a program Ole Miss ran over there. It had gone so well we tacked on the summer to the end of that year and spent it playing house and being paid cash to work at a bar on the Mumbles Mile in Swansea. When we got back to campus that fall, we kept on playing, and her roommate Dee Dee joked that I was going to have to start paying rent. At least I thought it was a joke, until Amina said that she really meant I should start paying.

121

My uncles used to say things about black people being too loud or singing in Walmart, and when I met Amina I know I probably still had stereotypes bouncing around in my head, but then I realized the sounds they heard as loud before were just a sharing of thoughts. So I started to think about how sad it would be if we couldn't say things out loud in public. All my half talk with my own family and shading the assertions—well, it was getting pretty annoying.

Mama said, "All my friends beg me for a copy of Grandmamma's recipe. She feels far away now, especially during the holidays." Mama had a butcher board put in during the past year and seemed to enjoy dicing up the celery on it. "It's nice to have her food. The recipe written out all neat, in her handwriting. You remember her telling you to 'Practice your letters.' Eventually, she had to two-time the recipe. Look at the way she writes. Her math is so feminine."

"Real butter. The healthy choice," I said. The men were loud again in the other room watching the Egg Bowl, Ole Miss versus Mississippi State. The Rebels were winning, where everyone went to college but one, a State grad, Uncle Jim, who would either spend Thanksgivings boasting or looking glum. I found myself seeing the house through Amina's eyes, noticing my family's quirks and imbalances. State was a better agricultural school. Uncle Jim was a soil scientist. Why would the others have anything other than gratitude about his privilege to go there?

It'd been these uncles that affected the awkward invitation I made for Amina to come over for Grandmamma's dressing. On the drive up from Oxford to Mineral Wells, Mississippi, where my parents lived, I had gone over the conversation. When I was feeling forgiving about my fears, I told myself that neither Amina nor I were ready to do Thanksgiving with each other. It was mutual. I had offered and she had too. Both of us declined so we were actually in a great spot.

When she had brought up the possibility of my going over to Lewisburg, she said her parents would be serving turkey and chitterlings. She'd really laughed at me when I went all blank and didn't know what to say. I could see myself at her parents' place, the lily-white boy, swallowing perfectly prepared chitterlings whole like a pill from the doctor. I imagined myself pulling some bonehead overeager move like saying "brother" or "man" to her brother J.R. at the end of my sentences for emphasis, instead of my usual "for sure," some clichéd *Point Break* affectation I'd picked up somewhere. I'd said "man" once to her brother when I met him on Skype. Amina said not to sweat it, but I wondered what kind of thing I could mess up with a whole day with her family. Underneath that and even with the bit of confidence I'd gotten from a year being with Amina, I was still felt like the guy who had the wrong thing to say at the wrong time or the loser who said nothing at all.

Amina was great though. "We're all bougie now," she said. "Me and J.R. are having them cook the chitterlings outside." She'd laughed like I was supposed to get that, but I was still waiting for the rest of the story. When I said something nervous-like about going over to Lewisburg, she let me off the hook. "Enough to do any-way," she'd said, "without worrying about whether you're having a good time or get stuck on the couch with weird Uncle Reggie." I told her I didn't think of Thanksgiving as being a lot of work and she said, "Men."

I told her I had some weird uncles too and suggested she would probably not like my parents' house either, but *oh ...* the food. That she would like. Though, I couldn't quite bring myself to tell her full on about my fears.

We had run smoother in Wales and the first months of school, studying and dating without parents around. I was learning to say my emotions at an emotional volume. *Riding on a train with an attractive, funny person is fun.* Amina found my half talk annoying, the way I tried to lay out a thousand clues instead of saying important things out loud into the air.

When I first asked her to go on a trip with me, I'd asked indirectly. I leafed through a travel book at Welsh breakfast, trying out the beans on toast deal, and said, "Check this out. This Indian food place in Stratford used to be Ben Kingsley's favorite." And then later, "The reviews of this new *Macbeth* are fantastic. They're doing it in all the World War II gear. Maybe we can get extra credit. It says here Shakespeare plays end in three ways. The comedies in marriage. Tragedies have the body bags. And history is just history."

She had loaded up her fork with some ham and ran it through the bean juice. "History is bodies too."

I laughed at that.

She said, "These people like to shake the story up, don't they? Really, I didn't mean to make a joke about history but listen?" She wiped her mouth and let the napkin drop. "Dude, if you want me to go with you on a trip, say something. I don't have time for this half talk."

Why would she go with me? Slim pickings on her end, I think. The only other African American girl there, Erika, ended up dating a white guy, too. Although I have to admit, Amina and I had fun together. They'd put on some dubstep or deep funk at a club that the Ole Miss crowd attended and even without knowing the tune, we'd have something going on, me and her, in the middle of all the strangers. Even the other Ole Miss students there felt like strangers. I felt very confident in the next move and a general idea of how it would interact with what she did. I imagined the other people watching us—not in the way that my uncles would stare if she had showed up at Thanksgiving, like we were remarkable and somewhat threatening. In Wales they seemed like looks of recognition that we were in the right spots at the right times.

I'm sure the sellers at the market in Croydon that we visited could've told me about race in Britain or the Welsh could've told me how their language was almost stolen and they weren't getting the good jobs, but that night the crowd seeing us seemed to build up our energy, and we were using their noticing us like stilts to see over all the crap that a culture can make. The trip to Croydon had been well-timed as well, a birthday-party-day when she was homesick. My mother had taught me a few things. She made me memorize her and my dad's birthdays and the anniversary. Amina was on that list too pretty quickly. I'd remembered Amina's birthday in all sorts of ways. I bought this piece of fabric she had liked in an outdoor market when she wasn't looking. We'd been reading about how racism in Britain made these odd inroads where everyone went crazy over a tikka masala, a jerk chicken, or when the Police used reggae beats but removed the protest. New government textbooks and English only. I was sensing the remoteness of my hometown and enjoying the accents and languages, and Amina's hand lingered on a bolt of cloth with a Jamaican pattern. She had thought my buying her some gulab jamun was her present, but it was really a string of all-day gifts, and the next day my learning that sex was an act of movements but also an act of not thinking, the relaxing of arms and the sunlight and the human leg acting as half covers in the hotel with too much air conditioning.

The year had gone so well that it surprised me, someone pointing you out from afar and you look behind yourself and think, are you sure you mean me? Being back in my hometown, hearing my uncles' loud beer laughing in the next room, I wondered how the locals would react when they found out about Amina and me. The oddity that things that felt so immediate and clear could ever be in question, an oddity that I would use to validate my fears.

My mother thumbed through the cookbook. "Hand-writing gets passed down, you know." My mother paused and thought. "You write a little like her. Come here, kid. Write her sentence out and see if I'm not right."

"Just because I watched *Phantom* with you last night doesn't mean you can call me feminine." I looked at the writing. Grandmamma had copied all her recipes out in an old bank ledger. As her boys ate more and more over the years, she kept doubling the recipe, trying to get it right, crossing out the old amounts, four sticks of butter instead of two.

The ledger had more lines than a recipe needed, and her letters rounded out in the columns nicely. The book had a deliberate feel, a bit heavy and substantial. Good paper. Grandmamma must have been serious about sharing everything she'd learned about cooking. Amina and I had a women's lit class in Wales that talked about female creativity and cooking in the early days. I found myself paying this new attention to what my mother was doing.

I had retreated to the kitchen after getting frustrated with my uncle Joe. I'd been watching the game with them when he started bragging about his football records that he got playing for the Spartans of Mineral Wells. I got out the old annual and turned to the football team and was trying to drop hints about the all-white team and how the towns he'd gained the yardage on weren't fielding their best teams, including his school, which didn't fully integrate with West Side until 1970. I was trying to get him to put an asterisk on his records, but instead he just started talking about his coach, and my dad and other uncle were telling stories about the guy too until one of them teared up at the word *honor*, about what he taught them, and they raised their beers, so I put the annual up and went to the kitchen. They had this common vision with each other that they would share by nodding.

I stared down at Mom's recipe book. She was humming a show tune; she'd been a voice major in college and her family had expected her to teach choir. She'd been good at business, handling pressure, keeping it far enough away so she could remember the big picture, the big path, she called it, "that could only be as wide as you made it in your mind." She'd tell me these kinds of things when I was having trouble finding friends and dates in high school, and we would go off to the other room to watch a musical when Dad had on the golf channel. And she would never need me to appreciate her eloquence, which made me more willing to. She hummed the usual parts of musicals but would also do different harmonies that I wouldn't guess would work until she pulled it off. She was doing Deborah Kerr's part from the *King and I*.

Grandmamma's list seemed originally neat; the recipes were alphabetical on the yellowing pages. Now there was a coffee stain on the writing, a splotch in the corner, and a grease spot under the word *cornbread*, as if my grandmother had been following her own reading, studying it, as if she forgot something and needed to touch it to bring it back. I shut the book and pushed it towards Mama so I couldn't cheat and copy the same neat font. I couldn't help but follow it as if there were a groove under a tracing.

On a sticky note, I wrote: "cornbread = four eggs, can milk, heart failure."

Mama read it. "Lord, help us." She opened the book back up to the page. Mama put the sticky next to the ingredient list and said, "Spitting image."

"Don't tell Joe that I write like a girl."

I leafed through. On the front page was a name I hadn't seen. It said, "For Lottie."

I pointed and asked, "What's Lottie mean?"

"Lottie. You know Lottie."

"Should I?"

My mother cleaned her hands on her apron. "Oh, she's from way back when your daddy was little. A black woman who took care of them. She used to have the cutest little house out back. Lottie and Pres stayed there. He grew corn around the land. Had some pigs. They say your granddaddy was good to him. Let Pres keep most of the corn. Nearly all of it, they say. Pres gave the family some meat when he slaughtered a pig."

My mother was almost finished with the dish. She shaped the top of the mixture neatly with a spatula. "Lottie took care of the kids when Grandmamma secretaried up at the school."

I said nothing. My mother stopped and waited, trying to gauge my reaction. I was starting and stopping sentences in my head. I was surprised by this new information, embarrassed, too, about my own ignorance.

"Lottie's recipe," I said finally. "We should say your friends are asking for Lottie's recipe."

"I see what you mean. I just always thought of it as Grandmamma's. I like to think of her when I cook. I'd never been anyone's favorite before."

"Grandmamma doesn't have any trouble." I point to page. "Right there."

"Sounds like I should have consulted you." She was putting spice shakers back in the cabinet, each one punctuating her sentences. "We could've researched it together. Found out who first mixed in the cornmeal."

"We should say it right is all," I said. "God, what is this? They had a sharecropper."

"No one *had* anyone. They worked for your daddy's

family. Don't you remember she came over here to help a few times?"

I did remember a woman, or at least an image of a woman mopping the blue and white tiles in our kitchen. I liked the way she was standing on a towel while she was mopping. I had never really thought about who she might be. She probably washed my dad's diapers, and what an awful thing to have to do and I never asked who she was.

"Look, I'm not saying you did it. But how much does babysitting cost? Can't we at least do better now? Tell Daddy he's eating Lottie's food."

Mother put the dressing in the oven and it clanked down against the rack. She gave the timer a hard twist and looked at me. "You do know that when your daddy finally sold that land it went directly to your college. I said I understand you. So why lob the firecrackers at me? Cooks always steal from each other."

I put my head down on the kitchen island. My breath against the counter fogged up my glasses. Into the table I said, "I can't even handle dinner. Did you tell Dad or the uncles about Amina?"

"You asked me not to."

"That was probably a mistake."

"If you want them to know Amy, you need to bring her here."

"She said she was busy."

"Did you ask properly? Sometimes it's more about how you do the asking."

"You think the uncles will be cool about it?"

"Have a little faith."

"I'm scared of my country," I said, getting up and

grabbing a beer. Mother had gotten a new refrigerator with an easy-access door where Dad kept all the beer. I took a long sip.

"Girls in white dresses and blue satin sashes." Mom half sang the lyrics as she reached around me and grabbed a beer for herself. I'd brought her back this cider from Wales, a *Gwynt Y Ddraig*. Over there, men could drink cider without comment.

"When the dog bites." I got her a glass. It was the kind of drink that tasted best from a highball. "Mom, Amina is her name. She doesn't really like when I call her Amy. She says it reminds her of a white girl's name. I must've used it so I wouldn't have to get into it with Dad yet."

"You should listen to her." She raised her glass. We clinked glasses. "I don't think they're as bad as you think. I remember Joe saying something about Pres coming back after the war. Pres was part of the push through France. But for black soldiers, jobs and the GI Bill wasn't too smooth around here, you know."

I could actually see Joe talking that way. He could get on a roll sometimes, and he was always complaining about coming back from Vietnam and it not feeling like he thought it should, everyone kind of low-key about the whole thing.

"Maybe I'll get that Joe tonight." I took a deep breath and started for the TV room. Uncle Joe was pacing and talking to his brothers. My aunts and a couple cousins arrived and were walking to the kitchen with their dishes. I raised my beer and told them it was my first one. My cousin joked that that was what her dad would say even when you could see a couple of empties on his floorboard. We laughed and I gave out some hugs.

I took a spot on the couch. Joe used the tip of the bottle when he wanted to emphasize a point. I noticed that the koozie he was using had Colonel Reb on it, even though Ole Miss had changed mascots a while back. Dad must have still had one in there. Colonel Reb was an older white southern "gentleman" who looked like a slaver. Growing up I never thought twice about it, but now it was such a clear problem, thinking of Amina seeing it, that guy with his trimmed beard staring off sideways, leaning on his cane while other people worked. I could hear the emotion in Joe's voice. He was talking about the state's pension system and the problem of tenure, and I thought of him turning on me with all that energy.

I asked him if he wanted another beer and he said, "That's what I'm talking about, bartender." I went back to the kitchen, took off the koozie, and put it in the trash. Then I arranged the trash to cover it up. I found another koozie that was the similar navy color but was selling tires. I used it for Joe's beer. I hoped he didn't notice the switch soon. I handed him the beer. The game was over and they were all happy but Jim, so I knew Ole Miss had won. Joe was setting up some bluegrass on a Bluetooth speaker, the Tony Rice Unit. Joe was controlling the music with his phone and was making everyone pause and listen to a measure of each solo, mandolin, Dobro, banjo picking the pace back up, then some nice high harmonies on top of Rice's subtle, deep voice.

"Now that is American music there," he said when the song was over. He stared and nodded to each person, waiting for each individual to agree. I didn't like the way he said *American*. It had a kind of walled-off sound that helped me understand and forgive myself for being afraid with my invitation.

"Actually," I said, when it was my turn to congratulate the music, "the banjo is from Africa. Have y'all seen that documentary that Steve Martin did?"

"*The Jerk*," Joe said out of the side of his mouth.

"No, Uncle Joe. It's a really interesting film. There's great music in it."

Dad tapped me on the knee. "He did a movie called *The Jerk*, son."

I was getting upset, talking loud now too. "It has this thing about how the slaves remade African instruments when they got here and used the banjo to play this rag blues gospel."

"They ought to talk about Scruggs. Man, he could pick it."

"Sure they did. But they talked about earlier."

Joe started scrolling through his phone.

I was loud again even though he was close. "It was about the minstrel shows and how all of a sudden these mean jokes by whites couldn't mess with the music. And so people stopped laughing at a joke that was never funny and started liking it straight."

Joe had my dad scoot over and sat next to me on the couch. It was not enough, I guess, for me to hear it. I needed to see them. YouTube was going, Lester Flatt and Earl Scruggs in suits and hats. I'd always liked them. They knew what they were doing, kept this spontaneous side to the music with a kind of program where they'd trade off solos, and they blasted out these sprawling songs in less than three minutes. I didn't need Joe to force me to watch them, yet knew he would never sit down long enough to watch the parts of the bluegrass movie I wanted him to watch. Sure, he liked the music complicated, with the mix of joy and heartbreak. But with his own neighborhood and family he wanted some simple story where he and his parents were only heroes. After sitting through it I said, "Yeah, they're terrific." I got up and went outside, feeling less at home than I used to.

Outside the fall air was chilly. My parents still had a bit of the land from when it had been a farm, and now Dad would only get someone to bale the little bit of hay and sell it. The house was set back from the road, and it got very dark out there without the Memphis lights up ahead and it was quiet, just the highway noise from behind the wall of trees. I wasn't used to that treed dark anymore. Wales had been open hills and sea lines.

I called Amina, hoping they weren't in the middle of dinner. I had to try twice before she picked up. She said she was stuffed and that they were done. She said I missed the banana pudding. She sounded upbeat like I should've been there. I couldn't think of any transitions, so I just confessed to her.

"I never told my family you were black," I said.

"You're supposed to make a name tag."

I could tell she didn't really understand, so I was quiet.

She said, "My dad said something about, why are you taking in the strays."

"What does that mean?"

"I'm not even sure. I told him he was crazy. What did your folks say?" she asked.

"I didn't quite explain things to Dad. That kind of stuff shouldn't matter anymore."

"I don't want to be a secret."

"I just keep thinking, who cares."

"You do, if you're scared."

I could see that she was right. "Can I come out there and get you?"

"You know, I don't want to be something you have to think about."

"I don't have to."

"Me and my brother were about to head over to Clicks to shoot a game. I'm going to do that. Look, y'all have a good time. Eat up. 'Bye." She hung up and I wondered how long a goodbye she meant by it. I could hear everyone in the kitchen lining up for the food. Most of my uncles' kids had grown up and moved away, so it was a couple of us that year. The cousins wouldn't have made a big deal about Amina and me. My aunts would just be curious to know more, seeing as how I hadn't had a lot of girlfriends. In my head I was loading up ways to correct them when they complimented my mother's cooking. That would kind of get things rolling. No, that's Pres's ham, I would say. Or, Uncle Joe, don't forget that the food is fresh because of the knowledge and hard work of other people. I heard them laugh through the window and could imagine myself in the dark, worrying so much about their actions and thoughts that I'd lost control of my own.

I got in my car and left. It seemed absurd that I had not left earlier, thinking how if this moment were in one of

135

my mother's musicals the audience would've known from the first scene what I should do and that they'd be impatient with me that it was taking me so long to know. In those movies, the decisions were not as much intellectual at all but the physical enacting of a wish, a movement to or away. So finally I was in my car moving from the crunch of the gravel to the smoothness of the highway, the trees tunneled around the road, the headlights shooting forward like a guy in a cave, head pointing forward.

I wondered if Amina and I would still be wishing for the same things, finding these excuses to extend our stays together in the same rooms. At first the audience would judge the movie happy or sad depending on whether she still wanted to be around me. But the audience would realize that either way made sense and was in a sense right. That me with her was the marriage-type ending, *The Sound of Music* bells and candles. Or if she said, "No, thanks, tiny man," the audience would understand and trace back to my most foolish moments, feeling at least that I knew them as mistakes now. An *Umbrellas of Cherbourg* ending with lots of snow and us spending the Christmas with different people because of me. This Thanksgiving mess I made, the time before when I assumed she would not even like the tickets to the Morrissey show I got us. I assumed that and then saw her standing right next to me at his concert mouthing the words to "Now My Heart Is Full," keeping time on her thigh.

Yes, the audience of this movie would be disappointed I had not moved further faster. I needed to hear it from her though, to see if she was even as pissed as she could be. I found Morrissey on my phone and put it on:

"There's gonna be some trouble/a whole house will need rebuilding." I drove a bit faster when the drums came in, the night all around, no streetlights, the dark corners leading to the creeks and the farms in rows under the moon. The causeway through the Coldwater Bottom gave a nice perched view of the water and fields and driving felt nice, like an instinct. Predication. Without antecedents. I was going to listen to the song until I got there.

# Dipper 28

Connie's dad took a second look up at Longs Peak through the binoculars. Connie had studied it too, a slanted tabletop peak, isosceles with a fingernail of snow in an outcrop shadow underneath. It had a nice look to it, and she could see why it got put on Colorado's quarter.

Her dad said, "The Rosy is up there, all right, the little red sucker. She's laughing at me." One bird they wanted to see on the trip was the Rosy Finch, a brown-capped finch that he hadn't seen in the thirty years of these summer trips. Connie had been on a bunch of them, and she been making extra time for her dad since her mother Donna died. Connie even moved back to Memphis to help him get back on his feet. In her mind, before the move, she'd imagined them in the living room, playing Scrabble, talking about Donna and what she'd meant to them but also about what his future was going to be. And him trying to help her figure out all her mess with her husband Jake. Connie and Jake had been on a break even though they weren't calling it that. In her dream scenario, her dad would end up less loyal to his grief, and he'd help her understand Jake. But it turned out that she and her dad were just roommates.

Her dad looked at Sibley's, the page with the Rosy Finch. "In the summer, it stays in high country looking for a mate. It'll be a lifer. And on her birthday." It was one of the ironies that they came out here for Donna's birthday, since she'd liked the beach more. Trips to Gulf Shores, the white sands, the tall dunes. Connie remembered all the things she'd find in the water, shells and crabs, and taking them to her mother, as if they didn't exist without her mother's acknowledgment. Connie liked the pace of those days and guessed her mother did too, but her dad didn't like to sit on vacation.

Her dad's trail maps were all laid out on the picnic table, and they had been discussing what trail they would take tomorrow. His mood had recovered since having to change plans. Jake surprised them by flying out from Detroit to the camping trip, making them pick him up and choose a campground closer to Denver. Jake was sitting on the ice chest and was bending towards the fire pit arranging the sticks in a tepee. His hair had grown out since she last saw him eight months ago. She'd been looking at him the whole way from Denver. His hair was graying now but was full and would curl around his ears when it grew. Maybe it meant he was being more relaxed now, less polite and more real.

When Connie moved to Memphis to help her dad, Jake stayed in a good job in engine design at GM. And acting the fair husband, he hadn't even had the decency to complain much that she was going. So understanding. At the time, his ease had confirmed she was making the right decision. Her worst thought was that going away had given him so much space they would just do this slow melt away or that he'd fall into some other relationship. Connie had always told herself everyone should do what they want, but

139

lately, working from her dad's house, missing Jake, Connie realized she'd been hoping that Jake wanted her and could demonstrate that in solid actions, like complaining that she was leaving the house. This surprise trip he made was making her smile a lot.

"It's all about hot air, folks." Jake balanced the last stick across the top as a joke and took a sip from his beer.

"Not as much air up here, is there?" Her dad was tracing a trail with his finger.

"That's why you got to fly in the experts."

Connie laughed. Jake had never been much for camping. He liked buildings and the city. He was an early believer that Detroit would make a comeback, that all the bones were there for a great town. They'd be walking the city and he'd admire a boarded-up brick office or the way the ventilation was running through a grate in Greektown.

A stream ran beyond the camp picnic table and made rumpled sounds, snowmelt still making its way down from Longs, the tallest mountain in the park. Easy down, hard up. They'd already added twelve birds to the day list around all that water.

She asked, "Why does it have to be the top? In the book the Rosy Finch doesn't even look that special. Let's face it Dad, you're not fifty anymore. And we're not fit like you." Her eyes were looking at the map searching for a trail that might be sufficient for them. "How 'bout that?"

"Ptarmigan Ridge? Not high enough," he said.

He shook his head and sat down beside her. A car drove past them on the gravel road sending dust in the air. He sat staring at it until the engine noise faded, and the sound of water and rocks returned. The guy had a dirt bike tied up in the back of his truck.

Her dad folded the map and said, "They pack them in this close to Denver."

Connie looked at Jake to see if he noticed that was a shot at him.

Her dad said, "I hope I get to hear our neighbors snore." He put the map back in his bag like he wanted it to say something else. He had particular ideas about these trips, and he and Connie had tried to time the trip on Donna's birthday.

"Must be pretty good spot then," Jake said, then drew out the words like the Larry David show. "Pretyy, pretyyyy good."

Connie laughed but her dad was just staring at the guy unhooking his bike. "This guy. From his helmet, he'll enjoy the wilderness at twenty miles an hour," her dad said.

Connie and Jake shared a look. Jake said, "With that kind of motor, you can look forward to about a hundred decibels when he opens it up."

"Can't wait for that in the morning," her dad said. Her dad couldn't fix things the way that Jake could, but she could tell how he deferred to Jake and got quiet that he respected this macho kind of knowledge.

She shrugged and said, "Other people like to camp too, gentlemen." The aspen trees were light green, their small leaves turning dull to shine in the wind. There was a bank of trash cans near where the guy was setting up and some sparrows landed around the cans. "Pig sparrow! Thirty-two," Connie said. Her dad looked up and nodded. They always kept a daily count of how many birds they'd see; each would guess a number in the morning.

Her dad said, "What a bird. So loyal to her habitat, such variety in her diet." The sparrow was perched on a bear-proof trash can that hadn't closed all the way with a plastic bag propping it open. Connie smiled even though she had heard most of his Pig Sparrow jokes.

He stood up, once again pointing at Longs and said, "I've thought about this for about three months now. Course I thought we'd be in the south. But me and Doc Bell, we're pretty well satisfied that the finch lives up that high." Doc Bell was a nice neighbor they had. He and her dad had a contest over who grew the best tomatoes, and they had a daily chess match. Her dad would come home feeling good after their meetings even though he usually lost.

Jake lit the fire, more for light than heat.

Her dad put his hands on his hips and looked at Connie. "I know how old I am, but by two o'clock tomorrow, I'll be at the top of that mountain. I'd like you to come with me. You, too, Jake." He walked over to a tree where he had hung a thermometer. "Think it will get to down to ten tonight, Jake?" Her dad had been teasing Jake all day about his buying a two-person ten-degree bag.

"We're up high, right?" Jake got up and grabbed two beers from the cooler; he wiped the beer on his flannel and gave one to Connie. He sat back down on a log across from her.

Her dad said, "I'll tell you, if it gets that cold I'm gonna have to sneak in that bag with you."

"Just shave those pretty legs," Jake said.

The sun had set, except at the very top of the Longs. Connie liked the way the sun stayed pink up high and glowed for a while until they had a fire going in the ring. Her dad stared back, and the fire reflected off his eyes. He splashed his decaf on the fire. It sizzled and he said, "Y'all ever notice how everything gets marketed in couples. Four-man tent, two-man sleeping bag, cardinals. I feel like that third wheel." He took a flashlight and walked toward his tent.

"Our tent is close, Dad," Connie said.

"I used to like hearing you on the other side of the tent." From growing up, Connie was used to his little guilt trips. They still worked on her.

"Maybe we'll hear a Great Horned Owl," she said. "It'll be square on your number."

He waved his arm behind him and said, "We start early tomorrow. Y'all don't have a beer bust out here." He unzipped his tent and crawled in.

Connie rolled her eyes at Jake.

Softly, as if telling a story, Jake said, "Tonight, I want you to take off all your clothes and lie flat and still on top of me, like a blanket. Heavy." The fire made his face look warm.

"Because women love to be called heavy."

"Because I want to feel you there. Proof we are in the same room. Not even one space between."

"Is it okay if I move around some?" she asked.

"How about we both move." Earlier, when they picked him up at the airport, there hadn't been enough space for a real greeting. Not after eight months away and with her dad staring on. Connie grabbed his head and kissed him longer than she had felt comfortable with in the airport. With her head, she motioned to their tent.

———

Connie felt more relaxed than she had been since the first months of their marriage. Her head lay against his shoulder, and she could feel Jake taking long breaths. The dull shadows from the trees and moon seemed to move up and down.

He said, "What if every night was like this?"

"Altitude sickness, indigestion from Donna's hash, conjugal visits. Which part?" She closed her eyes and wished aloud. "Maybe I should come back to Detroit?"

His head moved up and down twice. "I'd like that. Can you swing it with your pops? He seems more on edge since last time." He raised his hand and rubbed his teeth. The friction made a clean noise. "Does he have to use so much pepper?" he asked.

"Thirty years old and I'm still asking my parents where I should live." She sat up and put on his long sleeve T-shirt; he muttered a low boo. "They build Toyotas thirty miles from Memphis." She lay back down, her head on the pillow.

He put his hands behind his head and stared up at the roof. "They handing out the jobs down there?"

She turned on her side and moved her fingers across his chest. "Toyota needs you, Jake. We could live in the country."

He closed his eyes. "Listen." The stream was a low, constant splash. "It's so loud you forget about it."

———

Jake handed Connie a water bottle, and her father stared at his wristwatch. She asked, "How's the blood pumping?"

Her dad's fingers pressed against his neck, and he moved his lips silently counting. "One ten. Not bad, huh, Jake? I don't guess I could grind it out like you or dog boy." A young guy and a black lab had passed them a half hour ago. At that strong pace, they'd be at the top soon. Her dad said, "I'll make it, though. If that dog mauls the Rosy before I get to see it, I'll ... Are you allowed to eat dogs in this country?"

"I had some in China. It was good," Jake said and walked up the trail a bit.

Connie said, "We could follow the dog around, Dad, and check its fecal matter for feathers. You'd get to check it off. I'd give it to you," she said.

"All or nothing. Doc quotes the radio guy, gimme an A or give me an F. Don't care much for the in between."

Connie sat on a log and sliced cheese with a Swiss Army knife. She had already eaten her fruit and a ham sandwich but was not full. Their lunch spot was nestled in the trees, and a stream flowed ten feet beneath their feet. Her father had wanted to keep going before the lunch break, but she'd insisted on eating. She pulled her binoculars out and brought them to her face. A bird played in the stream.

"Dipper." She watched for a minute then handed the binoculars to her dad, who was sitting on the ground leaning against the log. He looked tired, and she wondered whether he should still be doing these trails to fourteeners. Walking two thousand feet above timberline was a challenge for anyone, let alone someone who already checked his blood pressure twice a day.

Her dad said, "Twenty-eight, that's Jake's number. Might have aimed too low."

Jake probably had the most energy out of the three. Connie called for him to come sit down. The dipper stood on a rock in the middle of the stream bobbing its head rhythmically, like a boxer, and when it saw some food it wanted, it jumped in the stream and totally submerged. It would pop out and continue to bob and weave. At first, the repertoire was comical, but after a while, it seemed like dance.

"Show-off," Jake said. He was sitting beside her with a pimento cheese sandwich. "A swimming bird, I like that. Look, there he goes again."

Her dad lowered the glasses and said, "Guess you're a bird lover now, too, Jake. Well, you got to love that one."

"What do you think it tastes like?" Connie asked.

"God, Connie, you wouldn't eat a Dipper?"

"No, I mean whatever he goes underwater for. It must be good." She took a cracker from her lap and frisbeed it into the stream a few feet from the bird. The cracker floated past it and eventually sank out of sight. "Better than crackers."

Her father stood, stretching his muscles as if he was ready to get back on the trail.

Jake said, "Wonder when they learned that? How'd they figure it's a good idea? Like that first crazy guy who found out he could swallow a sword."

Connie laughed as she packed up their trash. "Hey, it's good-looking water."

Her dad walked past her and tossed an empty Ziploc in her backpack. He was walking faster than before.

---

They took another break at noon; they were far past timberline—at least it felt like far—and the absence of trees left big views in 180-degrees. Connie knew that the top looked closer than it was, if it even was the top. Connie bent and put her hands on her knees, sucking in air. Her dad was taking his pulse again and stared at his wrist-watch. The three peaks over his shoulder still had lots of snow, but she couldn't remember their names—the three amigos, three disciples, something like that. She could feel her heart thump against the binocular strap, so she asked him what his rate was.

"One fifty. We'll rest for a minute." She sat on the clear area beside the trail, eyes on the view. No logs up that high, so Connie sat by Jake on the faded green tundra. A few wildflowers were growing, but mostly it seemed a desert, tall and vacant. Below she could see the different levels of trees. Aspen, spruce, and fir, the different shades of green like a paint store.

Jake rubbed at his temples.

She said, "It's the altitude." She scooted on the ground and massaged his shoulders.

"It's beautiful. This may be far enough for me." He talked softly, and his speech pattern fell in with her kneading. Her father wasn't listening, shading his eyes with his hand.

147

"Don't you want to go to the top?" she asked Jake.

"I don't want to push it. Besides, might be a good time for you two to be alone." He turned his head so he could see her, and she looked away.

She said, "That's smart."

He nodded and raised his voice to be heard by her dad in the wind. "This is the top for me. You want me to start supper or something?"

Her dad walked over and said some pasta might be nice. Her dad got out his camera and took a picture of Jake and Connie, saying something about the pretty couple, pioneers with expensive haircuts.

Jake started down the trail and asked over his shoulder why they'd been going up the whole time when down was so easy. They watched him for a minute, and her dad tapped her on the elbow, pointed to the top and said, "You think that's the summit?"

"Hope so, anyway," she said, and he started up the trail. Her eyes followed Jake down the ridge—even farther. Where the trees started growing was a clear line. One moment things could grow, the next they couldn't.

———————

She took a long drink of water and held it out for her dad. They stashed the backpack in a group of rocks off from the trail. "I think I'm going to try Detroit again, Dad."

He grabbed the bottle. "Perfect." He drank. "No, that makes sense. Wouldn't catch me around that many northern assholes."

"Jake is *not* an asshole." She started walking away. "Do you think I like being away from him? Do you even realize that babying you could cost me my marriage?" He looked out towards the view, and she said, "Look, I've got to give him another shot at being a good partner." She sat down and stared up at him. He was not looking her way and she lay back on the soft grass; the sky was an awful blue, astronaut, *Challenger* blue, in between some building clouds. "God, it's easy to get off track."

Her dad bent at the knees and picked a small blue flower, about the size of an eraser, and twirled it between his fingers. He gave it to her and said, "I know what you mean. Your mother…"

He was looking past her at the mountains. "Do you remember that summer we sent you to camp?" he asked.

"I hated that place," she said.

"We had to send you somewhere. We were having problems."

"Problems?" she asked.

"It's hard. I couldn't handle hearing about her and that other guy. We just kept fighting. It was getting loud, " he said.

"Shut up."

Briefly, her father looked at her, then his eyes focused on the distance. "It was just the one spring with him, she said." He talked softly. "There were letters. I never wrote letters like that myself. Maybe I should have." He looked at her. His smile looked odd on his pale face. "But she's gone now. It's no count. And you'll be gone, soon. Listen, you need to go. Stay close. Maybe that will help."

Connie did not know what to say. She had not

149

expected it, didn't even believe it of her mother. "I am sorry, Dad." She clapped him on the back but didn't know what else to say. He smiled at her and his face got whiter, like he was fading. "How are you feeling?" she asked.

"I feel great," he said.

She moved her hands to his neck to check his pulse, but he waved her away.

"Maybe we should go down?" she asked. There was more wind now and more clouds.

He looked farther up the trail to the summit, which was not far. "No, all the way now." He started walking up the trail.

She turned to walk down. "Come on."

He stopped for a moment and looked all around the big view. He looked down at her and said, "The Three Apostles, not twelve, just three." He pointed at the mountains. "Mt. Massive, Mt. Harvard, some graduates tried to stack rocks so it'd be the highest in the Rockies. Sometimes I wish I knew the Indian names. I don't know the name of those two. I'll call them Donna and Connie. Change the name, you know."

She started walking up to him. He sounded a little drunk, which the altitude and no oxygen could do. "Let's go on down, Daddy. You know how quick these storms are."

He gazed around and shook his head and did the top two buttons of his flannel shirt. He looked down at her, smiled, and started jogging up the trail.

She yelled out, "Dad, hold on now. Wait for me." Her calls seemed to increase his speed. He was running up the mountain like the dog and the kid.

"Slow down, Dad! Your heart." Hers was about to

bust. She was scrambling over the rocks as quick as she dared. She caught a rock and went down, scratching her hands. She could see him starting to slow, and she caught up to him and grabbed his waist. They both went down. He gave a yell, and it sounded empty that high. They were both breathing hard. Blood ran down her knee. He lay there with his eyes closed, his chest moving up and down. She put her hands on his face.

He pushed her hands away and said, "You're going to break my...crazy b..." He took a breath. He held his arm close to his body. It was red and swollen. She lay back, her hair on the dusty trail. They said nothing. Just breathed with the strong wind on them.

"The youth got no respect for their elders."

"I'm not going to sit back while you kill yourself," she said.

He shifted, putting his head propped against a rock. He was moving his shoulder around as if trying to get out the worst pain.

"No more taking care of me, please," he said. "Dodging your own stuff."

She sat up and looked down at her knee. "Oh, I'm dodging."

"A little."

With the blood and dirt, it looked like someone else's leg. Someone tougher. "Your arm okay?" she asked.

"Just a minute. Can't I just lie here, for Christ's sake?" He scooted back and sat up, trying to muffle a pained groan.

The wind was constant, but that was the only sound, as if the whole world was two people and rock. She heard a bird chirp and it seemed familiar but off. Like any old yard finch. "Finch," she said, but he didn't move. "Where is it? Do you see it?" she asked.

"Fuck 'em." He looked down at his arm. "That does sound like one." She could see him, writing the bird down when they got back. Boast of it to Jake.

He asked, "Why Detroit, for god's sake?"

She laughed. "Michigan is surprisingly pretty. The summers. The peninsula. You'll come see us."

"Hell no," he said and gave a short laugh. He wiped off his face with his good hand. "Course that damn bird would be on the highest place out here. Doc was right." He laughed and made a painful sound from the movement. He sat up, got to a knee and stood. "Let's go see it. Before the weather."

She helped him steady, and then when he got his balance, she walked behind him.

"Peninsula, huh? I don't think I've ever seen one of those."

"You've been to Florida with me and Mom."

"Florida don't count."

Below she could see the town of Estes Park in the distance; some of the lights were coming on from the rain in the valley and darkness. She always enjoyed views from above a town at night, as if the world was spread out in lines and rows, a human pulse. She remembered the feeling from when her parents had taken her to the Smoky Mountains in east Tennessee.

They had rounded a bend on I-40, when from out of nowhere, Oak Ridge hovered below the road, and she inched her face to the window and stared, her breath fogging the cold pane, and she thought the town looked like a toy and the interior lights of the car a cockpit of green, red, and blue buttons. And through the window sat the white, orange, and blue of the town. She had asked if they could visit the town, but her parents said they had already passed the exit, and she hadn't believed them.

They kept walking in silence. The sun came out briefly and then was gone, and she could sense the fast clouds. She tried to help him unscrew the water bottle, but he took it and unscrewed it against his leg like that was the way he'd always done it. Of course, he would be fine, she thought. All this time. And he'd be fine.

# Lucy and the Early Men

Santos said I shouldn't bring in any more charcoal drawings of Lucy to the dig. I liked making the early hominids naked with lines and smudges and searching for other mockups on the internet. These days there is an internet for every fetish. The latest drawing was a scene on an Ethiopian plain, Lucy Australopithecus looking strong, pregnant, walking upright, hair all over her body, breasts rounded out with the coming milk, the spouse a few yards up the trail. They'd been out foraging, that concerned frontal lobe look on their faces. She'd been eating plenty, but they were both worried that the baby would be born in the dry season.

Santos said I was enjoying her nakedness too much, and that I might make the female students in our anthropology grad class uncomfortable. It was true I liked to look at her in the drawings, womanly, human. The couple dimorphic. Not all animals have the guys and girls look different, but I was glad they looked that way. He with his cock out in front, and her with those wide hips. Brains were getting bigger even then, and the mamas were figuring out ways for their hips to let the brains get big, the head itself half the baby. The parents waiting forever for the body to catch up to the head and walk. I liked that Lucy's face had a bit of a softer angle on the cheekbone, as if, at some moment of surprise along the walk, she might smile.

I liked the way she looked carrying the baby in her body, the stretched-out poke of her own belly button, while inside she was sending good dark blood across the umbilical cord to her baby. Not enough is made about that advantage, how we are literally connected to our mothers. She was cooking up the good, fat brains in there that would one day put together a tool for digging up planted crops (you're going to know where the food is!) or an intelligence to figure out which part of the antelope would make the best water bag. I liked that her body suggested the intense work that it was taking to make a person, not hiding it the way some animals do. So of course she was naked and strong. Long fingers and those shoulders. She'd be able to hold the baby even with all the wandering and the climbing and the forests and predators, because, sure, it had slowed us up to walk straight.

Our professor finally got to the site. It was up the road from Rio Rico Bluffs along this path where the reeds from the river were not far off waving their long arms in the wind, the ripples springing up in the river and disappearing. This area of the Rio Grande Valley could get hot like a desert but had these nice tropical spots dotted along the river with old yuccas and sabal palms, recessed resacas from flooding where we would find things from time to time under the mesquite pods. Indians used to grind up mesquite seeds into tortillas. Still here in the Valley on a Sunday morning Latino families will go to the bakery and buy a stack that someone fed through a machine by hand, only corn now.

Most of the year it was humid and hot and so there was some moss hanging from the trees like Halloween decorations. The professor was out of breath and would find a way to make his excuse a brag. Oh, sorry I am late, class. I had to take a call from Switzerland. He said *Switzerland* in the way people used to say it in the 1900s, like Europeans were fuller people. I made sure to catch Santos's eye, to say, he does not speak for all us white folks. He would look back at me, as if sharing the mystery that yes, this is the guy we need a recommendation from. It was my second semester as one of the professor's research assistants.

The work here had gained an urgency recently. Some of the Lipan Apache had filed suit against the government because the Texas border wall went through their land, and Santos and I were trying to help by writing about it in the university paper. Santos got in touch with Gregoria Lira, who was leading the legal challenge. She was a professor herself, and with her mother and the community, she had presented a case before the UN that was getting a lot of attention. The wall was going through her mom's backyard, where there was also an ancestral path north and south on the river where the Lipan had always lived.

Santos was putting on his gloves. He gestured that I put away my phone where I'd taken a picture of the drawing. "It's like you're really impressed that she has nipples, is all. What's the big deal, you know?"

"I was just trying to be accurate."

"No. Everything else looks kind of fuzzy."

"You tell me why then." I was feeling defensive now because I had been excited by drawing it. I liked doing the shadows that cupped Lucy's full breast, the nipple out like a crater. While making it, I removed my own shirt and stared down at my own body and pulled the dead skin of my nipples. And so when I looked at hers and thought of the baby sucking on her breasts and drawing out milk, I couldn't help but put a little more light there. Turning water into milk. The bit of valley in between the breasts that must be right for laying your head down after. Like a pillow, a heartbeat. By then while making it, I had no clothes on either, and I enjoyed looking at her body, seeing her long fingers, imagining that it was her firm grip around my cock and that she was enjoying the look of me as I enjoyed the look of her.

"It's just a picture, Santos."

"It's the male gaze, bro," he said.

"Ah. Graduate students," I said. The professor was talking to his other research assistant, digging in his bag. It always brightened him up to talk to her and took more of our time.

"I'm serious," he said. "One time, Amarilis saw me looking at her while she was getting out of the shower. And she gave me a look in the mirror something fierce. I did not have permission. I thought she would bring the house down on top of me." He was looking down at some rocks trying to flip one on top of his boot like a soccer star.

"I'm sure one day I will learn firsthand what women don't like." I had beers with Santos and Amarilis on Fridays and they were really nice to each together. I'd grown up seeing how my dad treated my mother, so it was a bit of a shock to see how Santos and Amarilis turned towards each other while talking. My dad had his way of talking that I later understood as sarcasm. I didn't know the word for it then but I could feel the odd tone and the way my mother's face and body would change when he was like that. These undermining little comments. They were not even memorable in substance but had precision and surprise, like a paper cut, going through a stack casually in your day and then snap, there is blood and you feel it for two days. Death by paper cuts, so when she finally left him, her face got happy again, and he seemed to put his shit together too with the next woman. I think my dad would have preferred it if my mother had remained unemployed as she had been when they got married and had a baby. His next wife was a homemaker, and Dad was relaxed around her and not all sly hyper.

Looking at Santos and Amarilis you could embrace a theory that humans work better in couples, splitting up the labor. Before, I'd been more on the "humans are animals" and all this marriage and family stuff is for the swans. Beavers do it. Wolves do it. Even the gibbons in the trees do it. Lately though, I was wanting something like what Santos and Amarilis had, how they were careful and kind, and how, like I said, they would turn towards each other and sit on the same side of the table, like they welcomed a similar view and wanted to hear what the other one said without talking loud. I would be alone on the other side of the table, a cliché living in a trailer in my mother's yard, a grad student, excellent at making soft-core anthropology porn for Tumblr, rotten at meeting a real person who would tolerate me.

Luckily, school was busy, and there was going to be the side work with the Liras, who were thinking of letting us search their land for artifacts behind the section of yard that the government had walled off. It could even turn into a journal article. Mother was proud to see my name in the school paper around a good cause (a cause at all, she said), and I was feeling a bit of momentum after just surviving the indignity of high school and college, mostly feeling afraid. I'd never had many causes, which my mom said made me lethargic smart instead of real smart.

Santos was a pleasure to work with. He would say something and then we would work and we would save up the things we could say to each other until something good came along. Then one of us would talk and it would be good talk.

Santos paused his work to speak. "I'm going to need you to take the point this weekend on the Lira business." He was better at monitoring all the radical news about the area, which was pretty hard to get at without the right Facebook friends, and he'd managed to contact Gregoria Lira.

I said, "Won't she be more comfortable with a fellow indígena, Latino?" The first time Santos included himself as a Mexican American as similar to a Native American and the people we studied, I was surprised and said something that hurt his feelings. I never wanted to hurt his feelings again. He'd gotten so quiet and went over and worked away from me and I had missed our chat and the creative ways he would complain about the heat.

"She said she'd make some time for us," he said. "She sounded nice, you know. You should go out with someone like her. I sent her the link to the article you wrote. I think she appreciated it."

"I didn't write all that much." Just a bit of history that had helped me understand the wall. The age of bones.

Finding the fishing gear and the boat evidence. A bunch of weapons. Earlier that year, I'd helped write a grant with the professor to study the Reynosa side. The professor was not all that bad a guy once you got his attention, though it still annoyed me that he really only brought his full energy on when talking to the women in our class.

    I wrote about how sometimes I'd get off work and go to Anzaldua's park by the dam and you could see the families on the Reynosa side playing. They were allowed to wade in the water on the Reynosa side, and one day I saw a brother and sister throwing mud at each other, yelling, "Espérarme!" as they tried to load up their own wad of mud. The mom was cooling off in the water too, jeans rolled up, talking to one of her older children or an aunt, and the dad was upriver on their side of the park tossing out a neon fishing net, waiting for it to spread out from his hand, as if Spider Man, before the net hit the water. Nothing and everything changing. A border patrol boat zoomed around the bend, on the US side, the agent piloting a boat with two engines with his knee. It had a rotating machine gun on the back and lots of lights. The boat threw up a wake and the agent stared at me and at them with this cold, bored attention. The guy stopped fishing until the waves died down, and in the article I just listed the instincts at work at such a place, how there is an intelligence in any body that pushes it to the best resources, and how it would always be there, thankfully, pushing people further and making sure we did not stay still but strong and alive.

    Santos was going through some dirt now, gloves off. "I do want to meet her. Thing is, Amarilis and I have something going this weekend. We are going to put some money on some land and put in a little shack. It's like ten acres, all monte. If we don't buy it, some asshole will put in condos or a Chipotle."

"That's a big step." I could feel myself, vigorous with the shovel. "She doesn't seem that into trees."

"She gets me, I think, bro."

"Swell. A great plan." I found myself digging harder and sloppy. He told me to relax, but I just cussed at a root. There was a thick one from a nearby ébano tree and I was pulling at it like a tooth with the back edge of the shovel and it just led under the ground and stopped budging. It seemed like it had been there forever.

───────

Late in the day, the side yard next to my trailer behind Mom's house was the shadiest part of the yard. My mother was making a huge bamboo ladder for a local art show. I was supposed to try climbing it when she was done. She and some other folks were protesting the wall in Brownsville about twenty minutes away. All her art buddies were against the wall, and they'd gotten even more organized when two of their acquaintances, Vietnam vets, got deportation papers. They were going to escort these white-haired men across the bridge even though they'd fought for the US Army and lived on this side of the river for thirty years. No one could believe it, but it was true. Mom was excited that most of the art at this show would be from local activists, instead of from only white Winter Texan types like herself.

Mother had changed after she left Dad. She used to be a business woman in charge of quality motivation for her company's bored cubicle workers. She sprinkled her talks about sexual harassment and good management with Eastern philosophy. At some point in her life she started believing her own speeches, wearing loose clothes, and "living her politics." She cut her hair shorter than mine and let it go white, and she had this revival burst of energy I found easy to make fun of but hard to outdo. Lately though, after the Lira article, the jokes didn't seem funny anymore.

I went to get us beers out of my little fridge. She liked an organic beer they made in Austin, and I grabbed a Stella.

"Won't it look unfinished with that wire?" I asked, seeing her go to the other side to fasten a rung.

"It will look like a life raft. Like David Copperfield."

Mother kept tightening the step. It would definitely be a working ladder. She hadn't been so assertive when she was a worker. She would draw me little pictures on my lunch bags, Goofy falling off a cliff, his skis all crossed. The way she was now, she'd sketch a picture of some kids throwing rocks across a wall in Palestine. The immigration detention center was only a few miles away from our house on the way to Laguna Atascosa National Wildlife Refuge, a big protected bay full of fish and birds. People like us from the Midwest or Canada would come live down in the Valley and take pictures of the birds with huge cameras. It would annoy her, though, when those same people would talk about going back to their real homes to vote for more walls.

"You still thinking of going with me tonight?" she asked and fastened another rung of the ladder together, leaving her beer on the plywood workbench. I sat on a folding chair. She wanted to go plant beans along the wall, hoping they would grow strong and thick and vine up the side of the fencing and welcome crossers with food instead of just wall. With enough time, she'd said the other night dramatically, "the earth swallows up even walls."

"Let's do it. Maybe we won't get caught."

"So, it's true. You've decided not to do the whole cool, self pity thing forever?"

"How do you make a compliment an insult? It's clever."

"I remember the boy staring into his computer for something for hours. He called me Hippie Haley."

"You have a good memory. I just need to get out of my mother's house every once in a while."

"The house is a neutral place. It contains only the energy we bring to it."

I pushed back in my chair, leaning the back of it against the trailer. I always wondered if there were animals living secretly beneath the trailer, away from the wind.

She seemed to be thinking and shook her head. "Frigid, you called me. As if that's not the thing men say to women they don't control."

"Stop. Let me turn the corner here." I got out of my chair and was looking at the ladder. She'd glued some violent-looking thorns on the rails to show the ladder wasn't a joke. The other part was leaning against the trailer, stretching up the sky, which was blue and clear this near the Gulf. She'd moved us to the most inexpensive ocean she could find and ended up falling in love with the people down here, never thinking about how hard it would be on me to be one of the three white guys at my high school. Awkward and out of place, of no interest to the girls down here or so I told myself.

"I'm sorry," she said, breathing in. She was a big believer in breathing. Always said it could steady the mind and that I was shallow breathing. She would say these things and I'd roll my eyes, then a week later, I'd be watching baseball, and I'd see the pitcher take a huge breath just before going into the windup, seeing the sign and then going.

She said, "You are sloughing off the lethargy of your male privilege. Drawing now from the well that is the purpose."

"Oh yeah, what's the purpose, Ma?"

"Towards the end of suffering."

I was feeling my old resistance to her and I tried to squash it. The beer was going down cold, and I could feel it going into my arms and legs.

"We do find artifacts near springs a lot of the time," I said. "It's where the people congregated, you know. When I am complaining about the government, it's like I feel something strong coming up in me."

"Maybe it's not complaining then."

She had more lines at the corners of her eyes and a long wrinkle on each side of her face. They gave her face definition that a sculptor might accentuate. Sometimes I had thought of her as a statue. Unshakable in some eerie way. But now I was seeing the tiny smile she had while she worked. I couldn't pin it down, but I could see how ani-mated she was doing her work.

When I was in my trailer naked, looking at the internet, it had been hard to understand my mother and her new asexuality. Perhaps she had cleared the clutter of her life. How would I know? Anyhow, since Dad, she'd worn that kind of low-burning grin as she directed this project or that. Her work, the art groups, the clapping at her friends' dull poetry on the second Friday night of every month, they collected into her life. And what did the edge of my sexuality give me, anyhow. A knife with nothing to cut. Maybe she had it right all along. At any rate, as we finished the beer and started packing seeds into a satchel and waiting for the darkness, I told her I was sorry and that it was clear that I'd been an ass.

———

When we got to Brownsville, Mom said she wanted to plant the beans in the city park where more people go, and where the government had put up the nicer fencing for the better PR. The first wall they'd planned was actually designed to cut through our university's campus, the science side from the humanities. This more mesh-type fencing was their compromise, and not through campus. You could see through this wall better and almost forget you were looking through fencing, like you do sometimes sitting behind home plate at a ball game. The government was trying to be smarter now to do the same things. Mom turned down the radio as she stopped the car. "I never pictured you for one to go out here with me with a tiny shovel. It's like that body snatcher movie happened when you were sleeping one night."

"You didn't see that busted-up pod in the garage?"

She laughed. We didn't get out right away. Mom was sensing whether or not we were alone in the park. I found it easier to talk with her in the car, not having to look at her but stare ahead, like we were at a drive-in movie.

I said, towards the windshield, "Do you remember watching the rerun of the Berlin Wall come down? You told me to watch it with you." My mother had entered my room and told me to turn on the History Channel. It was the old TV in my room from when Dad had been around. When he lived at our house in Nebraska, he'd watch football games on it, the volume down. Mom didn't like the games or having the big TV on all weekend, all the junk commercials and macho celebrations. He finally just bought this little TV, and it would be on while he did things around the house. When he left, Mom put it in my room, and I liked watching it, the dial stiff as you turned to get to the video game, the cable on top. The cameraman was alternating between a long shot of the crowds in Berlin and closeups of dudes with chisels. Regular people with sledge-hammers, their eyes washed in gleeful spectacle. I liked that the news crew didn't really know where to shoot because the event was happening in so many places. Mom lingered in my room and we watched. She put her hand on my shoulder when a person from the east climbed on top of the wall. He looked very tall with the camera angle looking up, and to my eight-year-old mind, he looked powerful and nice like an angel. He stuck down his hands for someone to shake,

166

left hand or right, no matter. My mom was saying, "Go, go!" like it was live and really was one of Dad's football games. The news voice over the pictures was talking about families split up and that's when the whole orchestration and the spontaneity got to me and I started crying even though it was far away. I'd never met a German person, but I was glad that the man was sticking his hand down and everyone on the west side was trying to shake it, and how he started pulling people up to stand with him, and then they were dancing to an invisible song.

It sticks out in my head, my first political moment. We were both weeping. I was very sincere back then. "With the Lipan thing, I am reminded of you and me, and I think, why shouldn't I be more like my mother?

"Thanks for that. One never knows if they are liked by their adult children."

"I'm sorry for that."

"What I mean is, why now? I've always been like this."

"I hear Santos talk. He had an aunt in Reynosa that he lived with for a while. His mom had some health trouble and so he went over, and he talked about the summer there and how he liked being in a city with noise and vendors and lots of plants. And now if he wants to see her or her him, they have to pass that wall. That ugly fucking symbol."

"It's more than a symbol."

"I know, but he's my friend. I want him to feel safe and loved."

She was opening the door and reached over and kissed my cheek and was holding the back of my neck. "That's a start. I'll take it."

———

Lira's place was down towards Brownsville in Cameron County off 281, and I took the long way to get a sense of the wall's progress, and it ran more or less parallel to the highway with occasional dips and daps. It got closer to the highway, as I slowed nearing her town, the wall heading to the residential areas where it started bisecting the yards. One neighbor had his pony tied with a rope to the fence, an unlit grill not far off. Her family lived on the outskirts, and as I pulled in the driveway, I could see the eighteen-foot wall taller than the house in the fields behind. The slats of the fence already looked rusted and the quick light flashed through as I drove jittering like a silent movie.

While I was gathering my things, she came out to the car, jeans and good hiking shoes, and looked alert and comfortable, the way she had on CSPAN when she spoke to the UN. I told her it was nice to meet her and that I appreciated the things she'd said.

I said, "Santos and I really want to help you out."

"Oh, right. You wrote the thing for the college. Sometimes it is hard for me to go that slow in the way you were writing. Better to write a dissertation or poem. I think about my mother and her friends, together before the four empires and still here. It's a hard and beautiful story. A long one. And maybe one day they will be there to take this thing down."

Gesturing to the wall, we started walking towards the back. We got in full view of the wall and I could see it there, tall and still. The dirt of the excavation for the

168

foundation hadn't settled yet and was sloping up the footing like a new grave.

She said, "You know, part of your college, and I hope you understand my tone, is to work out your kinks, so talking about how much you are going to help us is a bit off. Nothing worse than the guy coming in pretending he owns the white horse that will save us all."

"Got it," I said.

"Advocate, sure. But don't appropriate." Part of the yard was for sitting with plenty of shade in the mesquites and nooks with other chairs. Farther, she explained, behind the wall were the fields where they had grown corn growing up. She mentioned bringing John and her kids down with her next time. She regretted having to spend time away from them to have to do this work.

I nodded and thought of Santos's scheming.

She taught far away but she still wanted them to feel connected in the Lipan community. She talked about juggling being a writer, a professor, a mother, and hearing her, I was amused at thinking I could ever keep up with someone like her.

I asked, "You think we will find anything if we come out here and look around?"

"Probably not. It's a pretty clear case, but that might not matter much. We have treaties with the US and land grants with Old Spain. On top of this being our land on sweat and practice. I get what you two want to try, though. You want to do something, something concrete. As visible as the wall, perhaps."

"That's Santos. He's so smart, you know. And he feels it. In his guts. He keeps his mind in his blood and then it just comes out, the cold facts in the hot blood. I feel lucky to be with him."

"He is your partner?"

"Partner? Oh, no. Not partner like that." I could feel myself quiet. We'd been talking pretty steady as we walked, just the birds in the background, so that now the deeper quiet felt awkward, instead of rewarding.

"This isn't going to be one of those macho things, is it, where you are surly that I even had a thought, naturally come by."

"He's living with a woman."

"Oh dear. They do that sometimes."

"Not that it matters."

"Of course not."

"Santos wanted me and you to talk, I think, like some matchmaker."

"Oh yes. I don't miss being single. You do make dating sound like homework. I never liked homework. State narratives. Better to learn what you want. For me it meant talking with my mother. Taking walks out here."

You could tell the section they used to farm. It was flat with just the grass and some sabal palms at the edge. The fronds hadn't been trimmed back and were hanging heavily. I'd read that they had their own little ecosystem in the stiff leaves. She was telling me about the palms, how her mother made the government move some of the sabal palms while they built the wall. She said much of the old-growth sabals in South Texas had been cleared to make the *Magic Valley* better for farming, and other such mega-projects by settler empires. She said "magic" in a way that made it clear they'd taken out more magic than they ever brought. The sabal was the only indigenous palm in Texas, and her mother wanted them saved and made DHS put them in parks. The wind sounded urgent as she spoke, coming through the palms that remained, high and distant, loud then silent as if taking an up and down temperature. The path along the palms led back to her mom's place and my car.

"Thank you for helping me," I said and shook her hand, somehow knowing the quiet walk had changed something. "It's an education."

"Well. At least you know who is helping who now."

———————

Santos lined up the edges of a bowl we found the next week. We were in lab, and there weren't going to be enough pieces to really make anything out of it, but he was treating it like there was. I was looking down at it too, some triangle design near the edge of the shard, and I was thinking of how quickly a people can disappear, or be disappeared, or just swallowed into another people, and appreciating the survival.

We weren't finding enough to have something for each of us to work on, so I was watching his hands under the magnifying glass with all that good light around them. His fingernails were little moons, rounded and well cared for. I hadn't thought about my own hands in some time, the machine of them, just complained when they were sore. His thumb was there with the tweezers, strong and delicate, saying perhaps, "it is often necessary to be opposable."

He was talking more recently about Amarilis. "Amarilis was complaining about all the time I spend doing this. 'People are not bones, Santos.'"

"Does she ever say anything nice to you?" I handed him a cloth and he took it without looking.

"She's right, you know. We can put together this bowl, but we can't smell the food."

"I hate it when people are wise," I said.

He stopped talking, which meant he was annoyed. I didn't know why I was. I said, "At least she is keeping you well groomed."

He did look up now, his face a little sweaty from the light. "Sorry?"

"Your hands." I gestured down to his hands and he moved them away. "They're perfect or whatever."

"I like to keep it tight, I guess. I used get these hangnails, you know. You think it's metro or something?" He was annoyed and took another step back.

"Nothing like that. I was just trying to figure out your relationship."

"Well, don't."

I said sorry and then something about the bowl. It was clay and had these three extra rims that were mostly chipping off. We were back to talking like we normally did, but I was still looking at his hands, wishing I were more of a sculptor, and how if I were, I would be able to take some of the good river mud and replicate the ridges of his hands and the look of hair on his knuckles and the lines that showed his age and strength. It would all start as mud and then suddenly it would be his hands, filled with spirit.

I'd brought in some Hegel while subbing with the professor's students that week. He'd had to go to Austin, he said, as if it were the city of gold. It was a juicy paragraph and the students had really tossed it about in class. I'd told them about the look of the wall from the Liras's window, the fresh dirt still in crumbles, the steel rebar raising up brown against the blue sky. Strong looking, like the insides of a building. Only it was finished or the face blown off. Maybe there'd be a guy like me one day trying to puzzle what its language was. A space person looking down from the distance, holding this report of human spirit to the light.

Truth was, after my talk with Lira, I wanted to perceive Santos's hands in clay, let them step into the world like a cartoon glove, posed like a question in a high school note, carefully crafted, returned with sweat and perfume.

———

Santos was late for Friday drinks, but me and Amarilis were sitting at the side patio of the restaurant waiting. In South Texas, once we got through the long summer, we made a point of using the outdoors.

"T-shirts in November," I said. She looked up at me then back at the menu. "Sounds like a Jimmy Buffett song."

"I never warmed to that vacation music," she said.

"My mom never tires of posting pictures of the weather so our people back in Nebraska, shoveling snow,

173

so they know why we moved down here." We ordered. We'd been pretty regular at the new place that served Belgian beers. We would pore over the menus and feel adventurous. Amarilis usually liked the wheat varieties but had ordered an Indio that they were finally selling on this side of the border. The ceiling fans were moving slowly over us in the breeze. She was typing quickly on her phone, somehow managing it without clicking her fingernails on the glass. She'd changed the design of her nails, this interesting blue enameling just along the edge.

"I like your nails. You always go bang out on them."

She posed with them holding her chin, making a face. "My little vanity."

"I asked Santos the other day if you did his nails. They're nice too." I was glad she was lightening up. Sometimes when Santos went to the bathroom or something, she and I wouldn't know what to say. "Say, do you think Santos is still growing? He seemed taller the other day."

"Men usually stop growing at eighteen and twenty-one." Amarilis was going to be a nurse-practitioner. She had lots of knowledge right on the surface and would tell us things such as, "The beer you are drinking is giving your eyes antioxidants and staving off cataracts."

"Maybe he's just working out more," I said.

"You pay such fine attention to him."

I shifted up in my chair and looked for the waiter. "Is he bringing these beers from Europe?"

"My father," she said and stopped. She said the "th" sound with that bit of accent that made it come out like "der." It gave her speech charm. She talked sometimes about how the area needed bilingual health care. "My father, he cheated on my mother."

"Oh. I'm sorry." I put my hand up so the waiter might hurry along.

"Santos says it made my radar too sensitive," she said.

"We all need a radar."

"She would talk about him to me instead of leaving him. She would ask me, who learns the night before they have to drive to Pennsylvania the next day? My father drove a truck. Who takes extra jobs and has the same money? Tell me, she would say."

"That must've been awkward."

"I lived with the worry. I can see any little thing big now."

The waiter brought the drink finally.

"Do you think Santos will want the Westmalle again? Let's order his now so it's here when he shows up."

Amarilis rolled her eyes and the waiter looked confused. I asked him to bring the drink.

The waiter left and I asked, "Oh, did you think it will get too warm for him if we order now?"

"Do you want my man?"

"What?"

"Like I said, I can be wrong. But there's ringing in my head."

"We're buds."

She was just sitting there, waiting for more. She took the lime, drew it around the edge of a frosted glass the man had brought. She poured and sprinkled the edge with salt.

175

"Look, he's smart and funny. He's my friend."

She said nothing. One of the lime seeds was at the bottom, sending a line of bubbles to the top.

"I guess you could say I look forward to seeing him at work and that he makes my day better. Also that I feel a little blue when my part of these Friday nights are over. Yes. I do. We walk to our cars and they are parked right next to each other."

She was sitting there her head propped up on her hand.

It helped me to stare at the sugar packet holder. I began shuffling the back to the front. "Y'all get in one car and I get in the other, and there is a whole fucking world in his car and in his house that only you get to know, you know. Does he sleep well? Snore? Wake up happy or slow like me and sad?"

She exhaled as a kind of laugh. "I tell him about the oxygen/carbon dioxide balance of nose breathing, but still it's—" She opened her mouth and was smiling at me like she did with him. "You need to tell him some of this, please. I can't know and him not."

"Shouldn't you and I fight about him or something."

"Please. I know he will come home to me. I hope you will remain his friend. And a friend would say this."

I nodded and she started to gather her things. "Amarilis." Sometimes I would rearrange sentences so I wouldn't say her name wrong. I think it just made me come off as rude. This time I just said it slow, my voice shaking.

"Just relax. Nothing has changed, right?" She stopped at my side of the table and squeezed my shoulder.

She left but had to come back to get her keys and held them out like proof that this time she was leaving.

It was odd to me how a lot of things seemed to be happening, but I was just sitting down. They had a TV on in the corner. The baseball playoffs were almost over. The Yankees had a lefty from Japan that was hitting .500 in the playoffs and already had a homer in the game. But the TV people seemed to only care about showing ARod's girlfriend in the crowd, the camera fawning over Kate Hudson, the culture giving the proof of his hetero life a big old hug.

The real story was Matsui. When he swung at a low one, he would bend his knee near the ground so much it seemed like he was proposing, and then he would lift out of it and everyone would be screaming. His question answered. A no-doubter to the short porch.

I could see Santos coming in, and I was getting nervous. They'd brought his beer, and as he sat, I explained that Amarilis had to run do something real quick but would meet him at their house. He was telling a story about traffic. McAllen was getting busier now with all the border patrol around. I cut off his traffic story.

"Have you been following Matsui?" I asked. "He hit another homer."

"They need a lefty to get hot. Pettitte on the mound too. I tell you, one of these days these damn lefties are going to take over this country."

"I read a lesbian on Twitter say that being gay is like being left-handed. Like, that's just the way she is wired."

"I buy that. And of course they used to tie that hand behind their back. It's a wonder we make it out of school alive."

"They fuck you up in school."

"I had this teacher give me detention for speaking Spanish. Gay kids got it worse."

I took a long sip and drank the rest of it from the wineglass pint. It was in the right kind of glass for Westmalle. I could feel my voice shake even before I spoke. "Some of us just crawl into the closet. We stay there and try to reunderstand ourselves."

He was quiet for a bit and still and looked to the TV for a minute. I looked back too. I hoped that he was just thinking a lot instead of having trouble.

Finally, he looked at me and raised his glass. "It must be a relief to talk about it."

"Maybe I'm more of a switch-hitter. Like Mookie Wilson. God. I have to use all these baseball metaphors."

"Mookie. Whoever coined that name is a genius."

"Amarilis saw through me. Saw how I looked at you. Thought about you."

"She speaks her mind, doesn't she? It's refreshing. Every day I find myself more attracted to her. I really feel like we got a shot at this, you know."

I nodded, knowing that was how it would play out. I did a cheers with my glass even though it was empty.

"Let's go to the house," he said. "We'll get a growler and make Amarilis watch the rest of the baseball and have a night."

He left the cash for the beer and I threw down a tip, and we went up to the bar to order to go.

"This beer is like wine," I said, feeling a bit wobbly as we walked. "Maybe I better not."

"Ah, crash the couch." He gestured he would pay for the beer himself. The three of us would always take turns with the bill and it was his week. He put his hand on my shoulder too, like Amarilis had. I guessed that was going to be the extent of it and I could feel myself shaking again and I even had a tear come down, so I looked over to the corner TV.

He was looking at the man pour. "I'm proud of you, dude." The growler had one of those old-timey circles near the top for a handle. He held it on his shoulder like a mountain type. I followed him to his car and we got in. He had an old car and he used to talk at work about rebuilding it. He liked its clear lines and how even a guy like him could work on a car like that. It had a new stereo, and he had to turn it down when he cranked the car. He must've really liked the song. Sounded like that nice section of *Trompe le Monde* by the Pixies. I turned it back up and Santos said, "Hell yeah." I rolled down the window, a refinished chrome handle you had to crank by hand, and thought about how no one old enough to love the Pixies should be starting fresh, but there I was, enjoying the air and being at stoplights with the music loud and not having to talk but just be there.

# The Doughnut Rebellion

Not everyone in Oak Glen was supposed to drink coffee, but Tillman and his widow friend Morris could. Oak Glen was laid out with a large middle for the nurses' station and the cafeteria and a TV and the couches. From the middle, five hallways went off in the different sections. Tillman and his wife, Janie, stayed in 'B' wing that Morris had nicknamed the benitentiary. Tillman liked how Morris was always saying energetic things even when there was nothing going on. 'B' was the elevated care that Janie needed.

Morris was standing by the window with a Styrofoam cup in his hand. With his other one, he waved Tillman to hurry over, but Tillman just kept walking regular, figuring the gesture was more for effect. Tillman was glad to see Morris had been using his walker regularly now, after a bad fall that nearly broke, again, the hip that put him in here. He asked Morris what was up before he started to fill his coffee.

"No doughnuts."

"What do you mean, no doughnuts?" Tillman asked.

"They've taken away the doughnuts."

Tillman looked up and stared, forgetting about his coffee.

"Watch the spill," Morris said, making Tillman release the spout.

Tillman sipped it to clear the brim and put a napkin down on the table, the napkin filling up with brown coffee. "Why would they do that? We get those things day old, cheap as hell."

"Nurse Deb says 'they're not healthy.'"

"Where is she?" Tillman asked even though he knew. Morris pointed with his cup.

Nurse Deb was over by the nurses' station talking on the phone. She wore pink scrubs and purple shoes with holes in them. With Morris by him, Tillman walked up to her, but she held up her hand.

She said "Miss" and "Madam" to the other end in a way that was rude. She hung up the phone and said, "Insurance companies." Another nurse named Jeff came from hallway 'A.' It was a bad thing to be sent to hallway 'A.' That was hospice way, "from which no man returns," Morris would say. At least they had not sent Janie there.

Nurse Deb shook her head and made a mark on her chart. "Looks like you old codgers want something from me, too."

"We want our doughnuts," Tillman said.

"Do you know how bad they are, Professor?" Sometimes they called him professor even though he'd taught high school and coached track.

"I'm seventy-eight years old," Tillman said.

She went behind the desk and pulled out an article; the title was highlighted in yellow: "Doughnuts: The Worst Food in the World."

"Y'all say everything is dangerous," Tillman said.

"Do you think a health care facility like ours should promote this unhealthy choice?"

"You better."

"Well, the health department doesn't think so."

Jeff stuck his head out from behind a desktop monitor. "Mr. Tillman, really, take their advice on this one."

"Now listen here, fella. I know how to choose between having something and not having something."

Jeff came from behind the desk and was about to walk away.

Morris touched Jeff's shoulder. "Have you ever had a doughnut, Jeff?" He gestured to the sky, as if that's where they came from.

Jeff nodded and Deb smiled.

"Well, then I don't have to tell you, Jeff, how delicious they are. What do you do to your fingers, Jeff, after eating one where the icing has flaked off on your thumb?" Morris tapped with his walker and brought his fingers up to his mouth.

"You lick it," Jeff said, tapping his clipboard impatiently.

"What happens to the icing as it rests on your tongue?"

"The trans oil and sugar. Oh, it dissolves and the grease travels through your arteries and clogs up some-where. Probably in your aortic valve."

"Melts, don't it? Count, Jeff, the things in this world that give you immediate pleasure. On that list, pick out the ones that someone like me can still have. Then come around here talking about clogs."

"I have charts to do." Jeff walked away down hallway 'A.' When Janie had to go there, it would crush Tillman. They'd had to sell the house to afford a better facility. He'd tried so hard to keep her at home, and before coming to Oak Glen, he had daydreams of some perfect hospice passing at home, no weird strangers around. But the Parkinson's got too much of her and he hadn't been able to keep up.

Deb said, "Look, codgers. It's not even our call. Talk to the mayor or something." Deb walked off tapping Morris' bottom with her clipboard. Deb, they'd long since decided, was the prettiest nurse, as well as the nicest.

He knew even without asking that Morris would want to talk about the conversation over another cup. Tillman had never had a best friend that was black; that he did now proved to him that even old men could learn new things.

Tillman felt excited, but it wasn't from the coffee, which he'd always suspected was halfcaf anyway. Decaf coffee he could handle, but doughnuts were different. You could not decaf a doughnut. The new policy itself was not as exhilarating as the way it began to shape the trajectory of their whole day. Morris was the ground game. Tillman was going to hit the phones and started with a reporter he liked. He called and explained, but got passed to an intern, and she agreed to attend the movie night speech that he and Morris decided he needed to make. The woman said she was "sympathetic to their cause," which was not a phrase from his generation. She said she interviewed the state rep at the AARP named Judy something or other and gave him that number too.

---

Back in his room, he pulled a chair as close to Janie's bed as it could get. Janie had been sleeping a lot ever since they changed her blood pressure medication, but she was awake now.

"Where you been?" she asked.

One of her delusions was that he was cheating on her. She'd bring it up at these random times, after he took a phone call from her sister or after a long walk. He liked to walk down to Little Coldwater Creek and look at the snakes and frogs while he leaned out on the bridge. Seeing copperheads snake through the water, the sun shining up the water around them. She'd note some ten-minute jaunt of self he took and turn it into something.

That day, she seemed suspicious looking at both him and at the chicken and dumplings from the cafeteria.

"We've got a doughnut problem. Me and Morris are on it. You wouldn't believe these teetotalers."

She said something he couldn't understand and he asked her to repeat it. Each time she would try to say it louder and faster, as if that were the problem.

"Just take your time, Janie. Like Ms. Emma said." Emma was her speech therapist.

"You need the thunder lady?" Janie said, slower this time and normal.

Tillman laughed. That had been what the students called her back then when she was tough ... or the calculus she was teaching was tough.

"No, this may turn out easy. But keep her geared up. You ready to go find the ducks?" They started the process. A fresh set of her clothes. He was eating the rest of her food as he helped. Shoes were surprisingly hard to put on for someone else, especially when she started "helping." He tried to maneuver her toe inside the sock but she was spreading it out wide for some reason. Her wheelchair was next and out to the fountain out front. One day they'd seen some mallards and some little chicks bathing in it. They'd never had kids themselves, and both liked sitting out front, watching the traffic and the visitors and waiting to see if the ducks would show. When he first heard about her Parkinson's, he figured they'd made some pill by now and Bam!, she would take it and be Janie again. At least the drugs got half of her going. Without them, it wouldn't be a life at all. Still, he'd do things that surprised himself, like look up things, the water at Lourdes . . . Our Lady of Guadalupe sounded pretty generous. He wondered if there was something like that in Mississippi. Or he'd look for the reverse; see if there was a efficiency apartment somewhere near Oak Glen. Outside, with the new buds on the trees making the limbs look cloudy, one of them made a joke about the waters and the fountain and they laughed. She said she enjoyed the air on her arms.

At first, it had been hard for him to slow down to her pace all of a sudden, like when you are on the interstate and going at a good clip and all of a sudden the car in front of you is going a dangerous forty-five miles an hour.

He was looking at her while they were noticing the spring and thinking how, in just a few years, Janie seemed eighty-five or ninety, when they were only seventy-eight. She flicked some bread down and was pleased that it landed close to a mallard. It took it quick and clean and then was coming toward them for more. No matter how many times they were out there, Tillman always got intimidated by assertive ducks.

He sat back in his chair, feeling antsy for the next step of the doughnut project. He realized that his morning erection that day had been a forecast of great things. He woke up with nice full one and pressed it against the mattress and felt a sharp pang of it stretched out. He couldn't help but laugh and tell Janie to look at it, but she just had one of those dull, big-eyed Parkinson's looks on her face. He wiggled it at her, "remember the Alamo." One year they'd driven to San Antonio and never even left the hotel room. When she didn't recall it and turned away, he felt bad.

Morris was probably the most popular patient in the whole place and could greet these people, shuffling along the hallways with tennis balls on the front prong of his walker, ask people about the kids and still be able to pry himself away gracefully before it got ugly.

Janie said something to Tillman but he did not understand her, so he nodded and kept thinking. It was movie night tomorrow so that would help. He was going to need a good speech, and the thought made him stand to leave even though they'd only been there about half the usual fountain time. He had to catch up with Morris. Luckily Janie seemed ready to take her nap. He would often feel relief when she napped at odd hours even if it made the nights worse.

———————

He wandered around trying to find Morris and heard him in the game room. Morris was talking with Mattie the bridge leader, who had always been tough on Tillman. He'd had a hard time being beaten by her and Smith when he tried to play with their group. He went quiet as the points went against him, and kind of flicked his cards over once, and that's when she'd asked him to leave the table.

Morris was smiling at her and held up a finger, stop, when Tillman came up to the bridge table to speak. Mattie had things set up with one of those shuffling machines even though the game hadn't started. Mattie once told him she hated to wait for the shuffling so she had one of those machines; she'd said that sometimes all you had to do was adjust things a little when you got old. So they had the machine and these cards with a huge font.

She was telling Morris, "I did not say friends. There are certain players, cheap women who will not pay up. They'll trade anything to get off my books."

"Genius, Ms. Mattie," Tillman said.

Morris was about to leave when Mattie said to Morris, "Are you sure the sore loser should speak?"

"I'm right here, Mattie," Tillman said.

187

She did not even look at Tillman, only Morris. "You speak beautifully, Mr. Morris."

Morris was getting up, gathering steam behind the walker. "He's my dog, Ms. Mattie. He's already got the newspapers. Plus," Morris leaned forward as if sharing a secret, "sometimes they like things to come straight from a white man."

Mattie smiled. She had one of those squishy laughs where her face folds up when she smiles.

"Now, bring that crew around the movie, you hear." Morris was collecting himself and was taking his time like Tyrus the PT told him. He put his hand on her shoulder and was looking down like he wasn't in a hurry.

"I hear you, Morris. I always hear the slow-moving people in case they need my help."

"Walk like a glacier, dance like a bull." He dragged his foot through pretend dirt and that made her laugh again.

"I always wondered how that saying goes." Mattie started some rows in her notebook and setting up a game. Word was that she was between cancers and talked openly about not doing chemo again if it came back.

Tillman and Morris were doing the math when they walked through the main hall. He said the penny poker guys were in too. Ten plus two is twelve. Janie would make thirteen, Tillman thought, but didn't say because Morris's wife had passed a year ago. Not that he was that sensitive, but it couldn't hurt to be aware.

"What's the secret, Morris? That lady would never listen to me. And the poker guys. They don't seem to like people anymore except to complain about."

"I read about older men on a blog once. We're the untouchables."

"Blog. Sounds like bog."

"This guy said men have created an iceberg throughout a life. Layer by layer. Men have not gone out of their way to touch people. Or say much of anything, for that matter, about their insides. And so people do not much go out of their way to touch them either."

"The iceberg theory. I think it happens to me with my Janie. Sometimes, it's me that won't touch her. She begged me the other night just to sleep in the same bed. I couldn't do it."

"That's the ice, man."

"It's just she can't get up for the bathroom at night. And that Parkinson's is everywhere. The muscles inside too. Is it so wrong not to want to get wet? Or worse."

"I don't know. It's probably good to say it out loud. Maybe ask her. I never talked to my Alice enough. For sure, that."

"I tell you, sometimes I'll look in the papers and see some apartment for rent, not far from here, and I just want to go. I mean find a place to take a real break at."

"That don't sound like marriage. If it was about separate, they'd call it something else." Morris was leaning on his walker hard and was shuffling his feet.

"You take a rest for a while. No doubt, you'll have another five on our side by the movies. If I can pick up five at the meeting, that would be something for them to deal with for sure." Tillman was starting to feel the doughnuts would be solved too quickly and he would miss this.

189

---

It was approaching evening by the time he got back to their room. They had one of the new TVs that let you record shows very easily. Janie was glad to see him and asked if he was ready to watch *Family Feud*. She liked the ones that Steve Harvey did, rather than taping the ones from the old TV channel. She liked his sense of humor and the way he gently chided his guests who said a silly answer or said something saucy. It was the speed she was at and he would only half watch and have a crossword puzzle around. They ate well in their rooms on swivel trays, the small little touches that made living here so much easier than trying to keep her at home.

She mumbled with some food in her mouth and he asked her to repeat herself.

"Since when you like their roast so much?" she asked.

"I got to eat up, Janie. This may be my last meal." He told her how he and Morris were thinking of a hunger strike.

"Well, then it's *our* last meal." She was smiling a devious smile, like she was glad to be in on it.

"I'm not so sure you should do it, kid. You've been eating so much better here lately." Tillman had seen an improvement, like the extra sleep and rest had got her in an overall good groove.

"But I want to help. They can't have some old lady starving in here." She made herself look extra sick then smiled. He shared the laugh and suggested they get ready for bed. They stopped her meds around six every night for sleep, so he needed to get the train going before they ran out. He managed to get her settled and was pulling up her covers when she got that look on her face, predicting his withdrawal.

"Don't you want to lie here with me?" she asked.

"I got to do a bit of reading now. But you let me know if you need anything."

He went over to his bed and took up a book of historical fiction, but couldn't concentrate so he closed his eyes, the light still on.

———————

After taking care of Janie the next morning, Tillman went outside through a side entrance. They had a magnolia that was starting to pop. He gave the AARP number a call. The Mississippi office was in Jackson and, after talking a minute, the lady, Judy, didn't seem much interested in their doughnut situation. She started asking him about prescription drugs. There was a vote in the legislature coming up to cut the benefit Bush had passed. He told the woman about Janie's Requip, which ran about eight hundred a month, the same as their old mortgage. They'd tried the generic brand but the delusions spiked. To Janie, he tried to disguise how much money they were, since the money stuff would depress her. He couldn't tell her how much Oak Glen was either.

"I call the meds my summer home," he told the lady.

"That's good. That would play well," she said. "So you coming down?"

"Excuse me?"

"Look, the doughnuts are fine. Good luck with them. But, you're lucky to be able to afford a safe place. I've got a single lady in Duck Hill on my mind. No pension, scraping by. The government will send her to the doctor, who sends her to the pharmacy where she can't fulfill the prescription. So, I don't need the Habitat for Humanity weekend guy. I need the-people-in-the-room guy. Real voices carry."

"I guess that's an overnight deal." He couldn't remember the last time he'd been away from Janie. For sure not since Parkinson's. Most of Janie's delusions were nice. He'd come back from Dominos and she'd say a family of Mormons had come to her room and tried to convert her. She'd say it laughing like it'd been hard to let them down easy. Of course, it hadn't happened. Most were in that tone. This trip would trigger the infidelity thing. And they'd have to talk through it and get her back in this world, instead of the weird one that'd come into her head. "I keep hearing the song, 'I'm going to Jackson.'"

"I like that one too." She reminded him of the date and time he would need to leave and said goodbye.

Tillman hung up the phone but stayed sitting in the shade. He had never been a real political guy. When James Meredith wanted to go to Ole Miss and the Border Patrol was coming on campus and everyone was yelling at each other, he'd just slipped out of town and went back to his parents' house and watched it on TV, hoping he could get back to class soon. He was feeling something swing open inside but was wondering if he was too old to let it go all the way out. At the high school he coached the cross-country team, boys and eventually girls. He lectured them about stretching, how the stride can lengthen out when you really get it going. How they'd made a kind of religion out of just stretching your muscles a little more than you'd guess was good for you, how the sharpness and then the relax create this new finish line. And that if you could keep the center to both the stretching out and the relaxing and just admire the abilities of the human shape, that'd be when you could surprise yourself and thus everyone else, and there would be something new in the world that had not been there before. He believed it when he said it, but he wondered if he'd ever really let himself do it.

––––––––––

He returned to their room. He could hear the clinks and clanks of silverware from the cafeteria and was hungry, but he needed to talk with Janie. Maybe they would order in today on the trays.

Janie was in by the window. She had a little cup that usually held her meds. He was grateful that they took care of that for the most part. Sometimes he had to remind them. For a while he'd been able to keep her in their home, but he couldn't keep up with the care. The meds he could have sustained. It was a kind of regimen that appealed to him, every two hours, sometimes upping the blood pressure pills, sometimes not. Trying the Requip after lunch instead of before. He hadn't been able to handle seeing her fall though. And there was the bathroom stuff. For him, even though they now sat on a strange couch and there was only so much room for their things, it was a relief. Just knowing that some of it was someone else's problem now, and he could occupy more of the space trying to be a decent husband.

She was listening to a book on tape, a mystery series she liked. She didn't like books unless there were a killing or three in them. She was eating a piece of cake but he did not see any real food around.

"You look tired," she said and put the cake aside. He kissed her on the head and sat in the opposite chair. He liked that unlike the other residents their chairs weren't pointed straight at the TV but at the opened windows that had this bright spring light coming in. And the chairs would swivel to the hallway if you wanted to look out at the nurse and resident traffic. It's surprisingly interesting to watch the nurses work, and you'd find the rehab crowd wheeled outside their door clogging up the hallway just to stare at the nursing station.

"It's going to be more work than I thought," he said.

"I feel like the cat today."

He eyed the empty medicine cup. Had they given her the hallucination medicine? That one she only needed half of lately, since she'd been getting better sleep.

"Tell me more about feeling like a cat."

"Ginger. Curling my tail. I enjoy seeing you move around."

They'd had a cat that liked it when they'd clean. Like the most exciting thing in the world was to see someone take down all the books and see the person dust them off, even though they'd go right back in. Ginger would stand under their feet so as not to miss out and go back and forth between them, running on full purr, her tail wrapping around their legs.

"Ginger was a sweet."

"Want some rum cake? It has a bit of cinnamon, or is it nutmeg? Which one is—"

"It's chicken pot pie for lunch, Janie, you want some?" He could see he was hurting her feelings interrupting. This was something that they were in constant negotiation over. How patient he could be with her, knowing she felt more satisfied if she got to take her time to do it right by herself. Thoughts too. If they came out slow, or if he could finish the sentence faster, it was tempting just to finish it.

"What I was trying to say ... " She looked at him like he'd punished the wrong student. Sometimes the students were right, but sometimes they just couldn't admit to mistakes. "It reminded me of London. The real Cuban rum. It was so delicious. I can close my eyes and feel the quietest burn in my throat, the kind of coconut on my tongue." She opened her eyes, still pleased. "You with a cigar you'd picked out, individually wrapped, showing me how to twirl the ashes away properly. It all made me want to dance or do something wonderful."

"That place didn't even have music. They wanted it quiet enough to talk." They'd always enjoyed travel, being with each other, finally turning from busy life and to each other again and looking, but also being extensions of themselves with all the new things around them.

She said, "You can dance without music."

195

"I never knew you wanted to."

"I didn't mean dance with you." They both laughed. He could see she was dreaming of her old self. They'd taken some students over during the summer but had stayed an extra week by themselves. They'd been around forty. She must be thinking of her legs and arms at forty and how you could do exact things without ever thinking of them. He was thinking of her legs too and hands. Cut a steak; handle a glass (a nice one that would break if you dropped it) with no straw at all. Things so natural that people forget the advanced machinery behind it. And of course dancing where you can even hook up one machine to another. How after something like that it is perfectly natural and easy to make love.

"Janie, I may get myself in a bigger mess than this doughnut thing."

"You never liked a mess." She started in her voice for him, "Let's get this show on the road. We can't change the world until we make our bed." She got up and went to his bed and started making it. It would take her a while to finish.

"Left up to you, the beds would always be unmade."

"I like seeing it undone. Like it's not off limits. That you could still crawl back in if you got a minute."

"I'm going to have to go to Jackson."

"Jackson?" She'd paused, the pillow hanging in her hands.

"Jackson."

"Jackson?"

"The town. The capital. We're going to speak to the people down there."

"We?"

"The AARP folks. I talked with them. I don't know the full story yet."

"The AARP. Like a whole team." She was resting now against the bed, a tall one that would ease you down.

"I don't know. I know Ms. Judy will be there. She's in charge."

"Judy? Like big tits Judy."

"Janie, don't be rude. She is the lead organizer over there."

For sure, she was changing into another kind of stance. She shuffled over to her bed and was looking back at him like he might leap at her.

He said, "She has lots of contacts you know ... does this kind of thing all the time."

"I'll bet."

"Janie, wait now. Be right."

"So that's what you want? Leave me here while you go off to your vacation with Ms. Judy. Would you please rub my back, Ms. Judy? Wasn't that a grand office, Ms. Judy? The wine here is exquisite."

"I'm going to go get some food. I'll get you something good. But Janie . . . stop. It's me here." She was still looking at him from a slant. She used to be able to hide her feelings pretty well. It helps to hold some back, even from a spouse. When she got in this stance, it was like everything he'd say would feed it more.

"You owe me a dance, Janie. I may have to step down the street to get a little rum to nip at tonight and celebrate. And then that dance, okay."

197

She did not answer him but started to crawl into her bed.

————

Seven PM. The movie would almost be over. He was late. Janie got it in her head that she had to go even though it was her bedtime. She was actually hurt that he could imagine speaking without her there. It meant combing her hair, finding a shirt she liked and the pants. He usually let her take care of her own pants, although it was excruciating to wait, to see her try to flip and loop her foot through the leg. You never think of how much fabric goes into a pant. And it has to be dragged up, against gravity and then buttoned. Don't get me started on buttons, he thought. They were like things sent to torture her. Finally he just took over.

"I like this shirt," she said. "Thanks." She was in her wheelchair, slumping and tired but looking at herself in the mirror. He had to look right too, but he'd hardly had a chance to check, since she'd insisted on going. He wheeled her down the hall quicker than usual and she made a kid noise of enjoyment. He decided he should not be mad at her and so popped a bit of a wheelie that she liked when he warned her. He was trying to remember the progression of thoughts he'd jotted down.

In the assembly room, the lights were dim, and the people that were still awake were paying attention with that movie look on their faces, all washed in bluish light. He snuck to the back with Janie, wheeling her against the wall. He stood against the back wall looking for the reporter he'd missed meeting being late. He saw what must be her, a twenty-year-old just checking out the movie in between looking at her phone, more blue light flashing up. The movie was taking forever. *The Sting*. One he liked. He liked the even older movies that were much shorter, where the point gets made and you know it and then the movie is over. Sometime around *The Sting* they got longer on purpose. He was bouncing his shoulder against the wall. It finally ended with the great loud pianos and all the guys smiling at each other.

Morris turned up the lights and asked for their attention. "I invited some of y'all here tonight to join our club." He did the swiping the nose conspiracy gesture from the movie. "Y'all remember that Wendy's commercial, 'where's the beef?'"

A couple of people laughed.

"I get out to the cafeteria the other day, and we ain't got doughnuts. Where's my pastry, I ask? That flaky, juicy, falling on the floor, bit of my morning. Yes sir, they took them and said they had a right to. So you know me, I sicced my dog on them. Y'all know Marty Tillman. The professor. He's been talkin' this up and he's got a plan. But it's on us too. The dogs got to run together, you know. So listen up."

When Tillman shook Morris's hand, it was smaller and more delicate than he'd have guessed. The hand of a surgeon, slightly cool. He drew Morris in for hug and backslap and it must've surprised Morris, who laughed and gave him a welcome gesture to step behind the long table.

The room got quiet and Tillman nodded to several people who looked up at him, still sitting. For the first few rows, they'd built in comfortable movie theater-like seats and then there were folding chairs in the behind and to the side. It looked like even their eyes were tilted up and bright and Tillman let the pause settle in. It was a trick from teaching. People now think that every moment needs a sound but he learned long ago that the interest lies in the variation. "John, Ella. Hilda Johnson is here from the paper," Tillman said and she half-stood and waved and sat back down.

He continued, "You are all going to be famous."

"Quit stalling," Mattie said. She was leaning in her chair and had a toothpick in her hand like a tiny wand.

"There is a woman who knows what she wants." Tillman tossed his notes on the table in front of him. "I don't need to tell you about all these rules and the committees that created this problem. We certainly don't need to make a bunch of committees to decide if this is right or wrong. All we have to do is listen to our hearts. But how do we tell these invisible people what is in our hearts?

"It seems, here, everything has its schedule. Sleep, bathing, eating. There are some days that I make myself wait for the schedule to start." A few people nodded. "I sit up at four AM and wait for five. I say, self, people do not wake up at four AM and you are a person.

"And I know it is just a doughnut; it's not even that; it's what the doughnut tells us. 'You,' they say, 'you, old timers ... you are not real people like the rest of us. You cannot effectively choose what to put in your bodies. Feed on your prunes. Suck at that rice cake. Enjoy it.' Well, no, damn it."

He slammed his fist. Perhaps it was staged but he felt himself swell with the faces in the room. Nurse Deb drifted into the room, a chart in her hands. He was glad she would hear it and report it from their angle.

"We know how to live too, even if the invisibles don't think we do." He was looking at Deb. It made him feel more brazen to see someone in a uniform. "Even if they want to hide us in here, so they don't have to see what it looks like to be old. Well, let's show them."

Morris said amen like at church.

"They think we're all huddled up in this shelter they built us—useless, a pair of old shoes. But that's not how I feel. I feel like dancing." He gave his hands a little lilt. And here was the pause, long enough for them to remember dancing. He looked over to Janie in the back. She saw him looking for her and gave him a thumbs up.

"We can take them on. Me and Morris, we're like Butch and Sundance. Are we going to crouch down, hide out forever?"

Morris and others said, "No sir." Or "Tell it," or were just nodding their heads.

"Are we going to come out with our hands up over our head, legs spread, and polite?"

Lots were speaking. Tillman heard, "Not this time."

"Let's show them we got our guns loaded. Our heads high, like we know something." People were glad now and even standing and pointing at each other. One of the poker guys had his hand like a gun, blowing at the barrel. Tillman held up his hand for quiet, but he did not really want it quiet. It was not necessary for them to hear words. It was just the swell they needed to hear, the crescendo, the top of the wave. "Here and now, we agree not to eat again. Not until we eat doughnuts."

———————

He was not able to sleep that night with thinking about the possibilities of the fight, and what it would mean to him and Janie. She was falling asleep even on the walk down the hall and had fallen asleep with her clothes on when he got her in the bed.

He made himself a bath, something he hadn't done in years. He kept checking the water, looking through the door at Janie, who was sleeping hard. He got undressed and lay back, feeling pretty comfortable, although some sticky pads on the bottom of the tub grabbed his skin. They had a sign in the hallway that said three days since a fall. Sometimes it got up to a dozen, and he and Morris would comment about it.

He was so tired he let himself sink further in all the way to his chin. He thought about how easy it would be to let himself go all the way but how the body doesn't let you go that easily. He was thinking about himself and her and who they used to be. He got out of the tub and dried off and went to look at her.

Her face seemed flat, sunk as it was into the pillows, which were all worn out from her lying on them, her mouth open and darkened with shadows. She used to complain about the mouth breathers in her classes who wasted their youth and energy, who wasted ideas. It made them both sad to bring up the great moments and formulas in history —choices that people made that mattered—and the students sat there and yawned.

He sat on her bed, his legs crossed, a thoughtful distance between them like a doctor would have. The mattress squeaked and she woke up.

She said, "Alicia, is that you dear?"

"Alicia, huh? I don't feel like an Alicia. We met on a river, Janie. We'd been in class together; do you remember? Our professor talked about the Koreas. I was going to take you out just one time. But you saw me on campus with that other woman. Do you remember?" He smiled and it made her smile too. She seemed to be following him even in a sleepy haze, her eyes starting to close again. He got up and put a change of clothes in a bag. In some ways he wished the Jackson trip were tomorrow. He wondered how tempted he would be to go away and then to stay away, as if he could be like those guys in the Updike books to just up and leave, get a new place that would become the place where your mail would come and where you would make coffee, and where you just prioritize the day with that narrower easy focus. A to-do list of me. The bag's shoulder strap felt light, the wheels at the bottom pressing in. Luggage was something that had really improved over the years. The light from the moon was bright enough and he didn't care what colors he picked. Truth was, though, he'd never liked those books much, even though he understood them.

He finished packing and put the suitcase in the closet. He climbed into her bed and lay next to her, all pressed against her and the bed rail. "You climbed into the back seat of my car, very calm-like, like a psychopath in a movie. You asked me where we were going out to after we take Ms. So-and-So to her house? You were so in control.

"What can I say? That's the way it was that day."
She was breathing deeply. It could be that she hadn't heard
him tell the whole story or that she didn't know that he
himself was about asleep, but surely, somehow, she could
feel that he was there.

www.ingramcontent.com/pod-product-compliance
Lightning Source LLC
Chambersburg PA
CBHW032117020726
47494CB00007BA/2109